Free Time

by
Shaun Waller

I am dedicating this book to the loving memory, of the woman who carried me for nine months, then had to have me by C-section to get my ass out into the world, after had to deal with my bullshit for twenty six years, but taught me a lot of good knowledge, loved me unconditionally along with my brothers also my mates, that she took in as her own sons when needed, but she always picked me up, when I was down, along with other stuff but best of, all the happy memories we shared in a almost dull life, because I am getting fed up of scraping the bottom of the barrel, I just need someone to give me a chance to make this writing on a page to all global cinema screens. But if there is a afterlife, I know your looking down on me also watching your granddaughter grow along with your future grandchildren, I just wish you got to see her more. I know you'll be keeping an watchful eye on what I am doing, poking your nose into my business, like always but for good reason to give me good advice, if I was going to make a stupid decision I would run it past you first because I know you would always give me the truth, every man needs a woman like you to keep him on the right track, I am grateful I got a mother like you. I just wish I could express the pain I felt, on the 23rd November 2018, 21:50pm, when they had to turn your life support off, you was only 47, no age to lose your life. My heart has felt like it had been ripped from my chest along with my soul crushed, but I know time heals wounds also I hope this feeling of being lost fades, before it turns me crazy because I don't know what I am supposed to do. Should I carry on with writing because it feels like it's not working also hard to get it going, feels like nobody even reads anymore. This writing only started because I wanted to give you along with my family a better life, buy you a house that you could turn into a home, give you no more money worries. I just wish I told you more that I Love You Mum.

Hello my friend, I hope all is well in your life, don't forget to tell your loved ones, you love them mate because life is short, you don't know when it's someone's last day, or time you will see them. Got to spread Love along with Positivity. KICK negativity out. First of all I am personally saying thank you for spending your money also time on this, both currencies of life. I hope you enjoy watching the different stories unfold. Also remember these are just made up stories but I am sure you will find pieces of myself along with personal experiences within, you never know you might be able to relate.

<u>The first story, Bridge Street.</u> Who knew taking a bite out of a new restaurants monthly special burger, will make you crave a different kind of meat. Who knew being a vegetarian or vegan, could save you from being apart of the outbreak, but it might not be enough to save you from human flesh eating Z's. You get to take a peak into a life of a chef, that is determined not to be a Z

<u>The second story, Through His Eyes.</u> Having a mutual hobby could be more dangerous than you think. When they stumble across their next adventure, on a break from university, they get more than they bargained for, learning a timeline that seems like a timeless nightmare, that they can't be woken from.

<u>The third story, Gifted Hands.</u> You would think creating a time machine could be so much fun, unfortunately this one isn't, bringing back creatures, that are extinct for a reason, because their only mission is to cause destruction. It is up to Max, that gets blessed with a power, you could literally say the fate of life as we know it, rests in the palms of a guy, that believes he has nothing to live for, he gets a rare glimpse into seeing the world, many moons before, before sky scrapers also mountains being the tallest things on earth. As he is greeted by the interesting characters of An Essence Of Time, go buy it!

<u>The fourth story, Stand Beside Me.</u> Who do you call if you need a quick hit made, but don't want to get your hands dirty? This consortium of highly trained, self taught assassins. But when the last hit, successfully got their boss killed, what do you do? Being his right hand man for many years, now being trusted to teach his long lost estranged grandson with the assassins methods, along with making sure his bosses killer is dealt with, appropriately.

<u>Bridge Street</u>

<u>Let me open your eyes so you can watch my story
visually unfold.</u>

Take a walk with me friend, through the corridors
of my different hand painted, segmented front covers.
I get to know you more, while walking I describe the
concepts of the many colorful ideas I etched on once
blank canvases as we pass through.
   I say to you " Here it is."
   I grab your arm as we walk into this front cover,
sparking my story to life.

A frosty morning has begun during the middle of
the winter months. Christmas is approaching, people
are becoming busier getting presents for their loved
ones, spending the money they have saved, in these
city' s shops. George a young man, short dusty blonde
hair, with green eyes, he is wearing black jeans, a
black coat, as he cycles to his job as a chef in a
chain restaurant, that is situated on the outskirts
of the cities town center, near the river Cam He
has ear phones in listening to songs that are from
his biking playlist that he has made, while he is
peddling his dark blue bike, wearing a black with
red trim branded red tick backpack, down a back
street. On his left there are people' s homes, in
the middle of the row is a silver saloon car, pulling
in to a dentist clinic. On his left is an overgrown
stream, with a big backed television that someone
had dumped in there the evening before. You know the
ones you have to take the front window out to get

the fucker in your home. A Moorhen swims around the bulky plastic tele with its young in pursuit.

Beep! " Vehicle Reversing!" *Beep!*

Comes from a dustbin lorry at the bottom of the road, two men jump out from the cab in hi-visible jackets, wearing their Cambridge Council uniforms, with thick brown gloves on. George pulls in between two parked cars, while the dustbin lorry reverses past, as the Councilmen go get the blue bins, that are street side for them to be emptied. A smartly dressed young lady is leaving her home, beside George who smiles at her, she smiles back at him as he bikes off to carry on his journey to work.

George has stopped at some traffic lights. He goes to press the button as a black car drives past, followed closely by a blue car, he notices out the corner of his eye, a young boy holding his mothers hand going to do the same as him So George lets the young boy press the button, looking towards the young mother, they are both wrapped up warm for the cold day ahead, she has ahold of a grey pram, that is transporting a fairly big flat screen television in its original packaging, wouldn' t be surprised if it wasn' t her fella that got rid of their old television. The traffic starts to slow as the light changes to red, the green man appears. George carries on biking past the young mother, smiling at the young lad, to a bus stop that has four different cultured people waiting for their way of transportation, beside them is a pub but it' s a bit early for people to be having a good time in there, he bikes past on to M11 Road, if you live in this city you know it' s busy, a road that never sleeps, if you have tried to cycle down there it's as a tight a nuns c..., I try to avoid this road at all costs but if my bike breaks, then it's the number 2 bus that travels down that route into the town center, but be warned it can take an hour to get there but I'd much rather bike a different route, I can be in there in 15ish minutes.

George cycling down the path on Parker's piece, from mill road to the hotel at the end. He cycles between a few pedestrians, past an over flowing bin, even though it's getting colder, people will still go out to get pissed at the clubs also pubs, especially women, dressed in next to nothing, while it's minus 1 out, I'm not complaining I'm just letting you know what I have seen, he slows down to let another cyclist pass across him on another path, cycling towards Grafton or maybe midsummer. George carries on cycling towards the hotel, passing another over flowing bin with rubbish. Some of the shit you see on the streets when cycling, is mad somethings would make you chuckle.

George is cycling through the towns center, it is a quiet start to the day, but I amsure the historical streets will become busy when the afternoon following into when the evening hits considering it is Friday, most peoples pay day, especially when the students come to life. A homeless couple sleeping in a tattered green sleeping bag, under the entrance of a night club. That's not the only homeless people in the city there are loads of them you know why because the council are pound pinching bastards, that have no care about people's well beings as long as their getting money for the government, the people who work for the country's councils should ask themselves who are they really benefiting. Then they wonder why there is all kinds of different crimes it's because of your fucking greed, idiots. Cycling past rows of shops, that multi-cultured people are walking past or going in, a few coffee cafes have people in drinking or eating snacks. Biking towards a smartly dressed skinny geezer shouting "Big Issue!"

He stands outside a massive chain supermarket, I can't say the full name but let's call it S_burys, you can fill in the blank. George stops at S_burys, getting off, placing his bike beside a black metal bike rail, that has a couple of bikes locked to, it even contains a locked bike frame, missing it wheels.

He walks in asking to the Big Issue seller "How's it going Lee? Keep an eye on that bro."

Lee with gelled combed black hair with Big Issues magazines in a plastic wallet responds saying" Not bad, will do mate."

George walks in to get a drink along with a pack of smokes.

George is locking his bike up with a black D-lock, he takes his key from the lock. Looking down the street noticing his restaurants bins have been taken in. He puts his keys in his jeans pocket, with his rucksack on, that has his uniform in. He walks to the front of his restaurant which is called David2Marseille. George has also worked next door in Café Red, beside that is a brassiere called Côte David2Marseille is empty from customers, because it doesn't open for another two hours, apart from the kitchen porter behind the bar making a coffee. The other two restaurants on the other hand have customers in them because they do breakfasts along with open earlier at 9 where George's opens at 12, but he starts at 10, but at Café Red, you would start at 8 until 10-11 at night, fucking long shifts to be on your feet for, Saturdays are horrible shifts in both restaurants, I'm sure in Côte as well.

George says " Morning bro, I will take a cup please, make sure you sprinkle chocolate over the top."

The kitchen porter is from the Czech Republic, he has dreadlocks that go down to his lower back, dressed in light blue jeans with a white t' shirt on, his name is Andrej.

He responds saying " Yeh mon, sure. Chef is in the back, rolling."

Now you shouldn't judge a man by his speech or the way he looks, but you would be right if you thought he's a stoner, to the point a couple of the funny fags filled with the devils lettuce don't do much to him anymore. George carries on walking past rows of tables with chairs tucked underneath.

He responds saying " Oh right bro, don't forget two sugars."

George is walking to the back bit where more booths are, salt alongside pepper grinders, with a big bottle of chili oil sit, huddled on top in the middle of the tables, along with a steak knife next to a fork, sit on top of white napkin either side if the tables. Some Jamaican dance hall music playing from the kitchen. He pokes his head in to see where the head chef is, but can't see anyone just a mobile speaker, on top of a chest freezer. He carries on walking past tattered framed mirrors on the wall for decoration, also a massive clock on one of the walls, with black hands that are like a person on Jsa, they don't work. He pulls open the glass door to the outside part of the restaurant, that has dark wooden decking with plastic dark grey table, that have not been set up because of the weather not being the sunniest. He opens a light brown garden gate to his left side.

The Czech Republican head chef is rolling a long cigarette on the table, with a wink. In the corner beside the restaurants green bins, there is a building behind that, with windows equally separated, if you look over the bricked wall, a massive fall to the buildings underground car park with a delver metal retractable door. There is a plastic tub on the table with darts inside, dirty coffee cups sit beside the tub, on the grey garden table.

George says asking " Yo bratr od jiné matky, co se dě je?"

In English he said " Yo brother from different mother, what's happening?"

The head chef looks surprised while bumping fist with George, that is unwrapping his box of smokes, to flip two over out of superstition, it is supposed to be good luck, when they done ten boxes, it would be one for ten, two for twenty.

Chef is a skinny guy with black hair also dark eyes, he is in his thirties.

The head chef responds saying " I will reply in English because if I say in Czech, you won't understand, but not bad though considering your accent bratr."

George lights his smoke with a red lighter, which he puts the packet alongside the lighter, back in his pocket while the head chef licks the rolling paper.

After smoke leaving Georges mouth.

He responds " Yeah, Jackson has been teaching me bro, fuck I was saying this all night, so I didn' t forget."

Now Jackson is someone you will meet later mate, he is the head chefs younger bratr. He is a funny guy also a fucking hard worker, he is a good chef, just a brilliant guy to be around, positive vibes.

The wooden door opens, Andrej walks over to the table with a black serving tray that he places down, three cappuccinos sit on top. Chocolate sprinkled all over the place, there is more on the tray than on the foamy milk, but George won' t complain not if it is free, the best things are.

George breathing out smoke while asking " What one is mine bro?"

Andrej response is " Any one brother, they all have the same amount of sugar."

Chef takes a few tokes of the king-skin roll up after passes it to Andrej. While George picks up a cup, at the same time asking, " Quick match?"

Chef responds asking " Around the world?"

The battered dart board hanging on the wall that is beside the door.

George nods while saying " Oh yeah baby, let' s do this."

Andrej sits down on a plastic chair while saying " I will just watch this one."

George walks over to the dartboard, taking out the three darts that are scattered around the board.

While he says to Andrej " Kočička. "

Chef laughs while he takes his fancy darts out from a small black case

Chef saying " Check these out bratr, they come yesterday. "

He passes them to George, after he takes a sip from the middle cup. George is nodding while looking at them, he passes the TARGET DAYTON FIRE GT 95% TUNGTEN STEEL TIP darts back.

George asks " They look nice, have you played with them yet?"

He stubs his cigarette out while Chef is smoking the spliff, responding " Not yet, I am going to christen them now. "

George asks " How much they set you back?"

Chef responds saying " Should have been about 120 quid but I got them for 49.99 quid. "

George just about to throw a dart to get warmed up but is stopped, as he looks at the chef surprised, that is nodding.

George responds saying " Fuck that, I don' t like spending that much, I have trouble if I spend 60 on trainers. "

Andrej says " Same here bratr, I make shit last especially trainers. "

George fist bump in agreement with Andrej while George is nodding his head.

George throws a few practice shots at the dart board while Chef sorts himself out.

George lost the match of darts, I don' t want to make excuses for him but it' s because of lack of practice, compared to the head chef that has a dart board at his home. Drum ' n' base is blaring from the kitchen. George walks out from the door opposite the kitchens entrance, wearing his all black chef uniform He is adjusting his black chef hat, that has a white cutlery crest in the middle. Through the door that George just walked out of, is a door that leads to an alley where the chefs or waiting staff go smoke in busy times, also the office where the manager is most of the time. The manager is a Polish guy called Chris, his assistant is a French lady called Aida. She passes George while he is walking into the kitchen to start prep for the day, they exchange smiles in passing. At the front is the kitchen porter, who is sweeping the restaurants floor around the tables legs. George is rolling up his sleeves as he enters inside the kitchen.

The head chef passes George a piece of paper as he passes the pizza section. After Chef switches on the three tier stone pizza oven that he has just cleaned. George looks at the piece of paper while the head chef opens the big grey door for the walk in fridge, that is opposite twinned, deep silver sinks. Behind George is a six slated grill, which is sandwiched between two twinned fryers, also the pizza oven. The head chef reappears from the walk-in, while he is nodding to drum ' n' base beat, he passes him a plastic container full of burgers, but they are not ordinary burgers, they are lamb burgers.

George says asking " Yeah seems simple enough, bottom bun, squirt of pesto mayo, lettuce, slice of tomato, burger with guacamole on top with three crispy onion rings, closed with the top bun, on a tray with fries also a pot of relish. This the months special bro?"

The head chef is pouring pizza sauce in saladette big metal container, that has a 2oz red ladle handle sticking out from, it is beside a big metal container full of tiny mozzarella cubes, the cheese alongside the sauce act like a divider, because in smaller rectangular metal pots in three rows, on the left is veg on the right is meat, four fridge compartments underneath, next to the fridge unit in the corner is the marbled slab where they make the dough circular.

The head chef responds saying " Yes also there is a veggie pizza."

George slices the lamb burger packaging open, he puts the red handles knife down on the red chopping board. That is on top of the meat fridge that is underneath the grill. George is putting blue gloves on to sort the burgers out so he can put the lamb burgers inside.

While he responds saying " Oh right bro, I think the lamb burger will sell well."

George chucks the empty packaging in one of four grey plastic bins dotted around. There is a six burner stove to the right side of the fryers that belongs to the pasta section. A massive pot of water on in the right hand corner of the stove, which is for bringing pasta up to temp, with eight metal pasta pots hanging on the edge of the canopy. Against the wall beside the stove is the same type of fridge as the pizza section, in fact the grill section has the same type of fridge. In the corner is the kitchen porter section, the big dishwasher is currently filling up, a doorway beside which leads to two chest freezers which is for making desserts, which the KP does, he also gets paid in peanuts. Now I have shown you around my second home, but just for your information there are no windows or doors that lead outside, this kitchen has two doors one that anyone that works in this place comes in, which is a swinging white door, the other one is beside the walk-in fridge which leads to the customer toilet, also drink stock room I can tell you it gets hotter than Satan's nut-sack mate in the summer, especially on the grill section, sandwiched between them two boiling section for a thirteen hour shift, you're having Satan's nut-sack, fucking hell, George start to switch on the grill to carry on setting up for the day, now Fridays are funny days because it can be busy during the day to evening or dead during the day then at 6 or 7, it fucking explodes into life.

George is slicing cherry tomatoes in half, on a green board with a green handled knife, putting them in a tub to share over all three sections. The head chef is walking with a tray of defrosted pizza dough, to put on a shelf underneath the marble. After he sieves ' Double O' flour with semolina on to the marble into a mountain. George is sharing the tomato halves with all three sections, the kitchen porter walks in to the kitchen in a black chefs uniform to keep the kitchen clean also fill the dessert section. George starts speedily slicing hollowed out cucumbers, three whole, twelve halves, not even looking as he slices because he is talking to the Andrej about football. The head chef is making them some breakfast which is pizza dough cooked in a loaf, cheese on top mixed with black pepper, sliced in half, after sliced into quarters, some rocket with salami along with a couple of slices of buffalo tomato in the middle, trust me you have to try this mate, if I had the money I would have a stool in town, selling these bad boys. George putting the evenly sliced cucumbers in to a plastic container, that is lined with a blue food bag. George busting a little dance move to the musical beat while walking over to the pasta section, salt trickling from his finger tips, into the boiling water below, he does this a couple of times, after pouring penne from its industrial five kilo packaging, stirring.

George, head chef along with the kitchen porter are outside the back, having a break before the restaurant opens, George with a smoke lit, hanging from his lips, one eye closed to avoid smoke in his eye, looking like pop-eye, I don' t spinach but I eat it on its own. He stands throwing darts at the board, on his second dart hits bullseye.

He turns saying to the head chef " I am on two bro." George turns throwing the the third dart, triple two the dart is sticking out from, which means George is on five now. Chef stands up from his seat, stubbing his roll-up out after fist bumps George as he goes to throw his three darts. George smoking while drinking his coffee, sitting on the wall at the side. On the chefs first dart he hits the bulls eye. George says " Nice but luckily I got the triple two because I would be back in the middle. "

They are playing a match of around the world.

A ticket is being printed out from a black ticket machine that is next to some burger trays that are already lined with branded tracing paper, which are white with the green company's logo on, dotted around. George's hand takes the paper from the machine, putting it in a grey ticket holder strip. For starters it is just mozzarella garlic bread, which the head chef starts making. Followed by two burgers, which George is slapping on the grill as I speak.

The head chef with his back to George, says " I found an old music artist you will like bratr, I will put him on. "

The chef scoops up the raw mozzarella bread, putting it inside the pizza oven with the silver pizza scoop, the pizza oven is currently three hundred thirty seven degrees. George is setting up a tray for the burgers, while over his left shoulder the pink burger are sizzling on the grill. He puts three quartered gherkins in the middle, fills up a dark brown pot of burger relish, putting it beside the gherkins. After he gets the sliced in half burger buns, toasting them in the grill until they have the square grill marks, putting the bottom bun on the tray with the top leaning up against the tray. After he puts burger sauce on the bottom bun, squashing it down with lettuce also a slice of buffalo tomato. The chef is flicking through his mobile, putting it on the side while a song starts to play. George turns the burger to the side with the spatula, making the square grill marks.

After he asks the head chef " Who is this?"

The head chef taking the bread out from the oven, onto a a wooden board, he slices into six quarters with the pizza slice, after pressing a black door bell to get a waitress or waiters to take the food.

The chef responds saying " Rodriguez -Street Boy. "

The assistant manager comes in quickly taking the food after leaving. Oh yeah I forgot to tell you that George won the game of darts, so for today they are on one-all.

George says asking " I Like this guy, you think he is still alive?"

The head chef responds saying " No bro I think he is dead, I have one of his albums, I will put it on. "

George turns the burgers on the grill, revealing nice squared grill marks as the other side starts to sizzle.

After a busy lunch service, all the customers have been fed, paid to leave. George is sitting next to a white door on his break, eating a pepperoni pizza with BBQ sauce drizzled over the top. He has a cup of coffee beside with an open A4 lined notepad with a black inked pen in his hand, he is writing, with the other hand he is eating slices of the pizza, he is nodding to a musician playing within his headphones.

George is putting his plate back in the kitchen, the kitchen porter has gone home, more staff will be in for the evening shift.

George says " Thanks brother for the pizza, it was sexy. "

The head chef responds asking " Your welcome brother, quick smoke also game?"

George takes a sip of his coffee after nods in agreement, they both leave the kitchen. The assistant manager is walking towards them, asking George " Can I have a cigarette please?"

George takes his packet of cigarettes from his pocket, taking one out, giving her one, along with a cigarette, I wink but of course I am joking, he never gave her a cigarette, only joking anyway she takes the cigarette from George's fingers. While the head chef holds the glass door open for them

George is back from lunch, while the head chef has gone for his lunch, the restaurant is empty which is usually the case between the hours of three to six in the afternoon. Some music is playing while George with blue gloves on, is putting some grated cheddar from a full container into half blue bags, on red scales as they read different numbers each time but have be close to eighty grams, he will split the full container in half, eighty grams which is for the Haddock risotto, the other half will be forty grams that is for the Cobb salad. Jackson walks in to the kitchen, wearing his casual clothes but George doesn't notice him, too busy dividing the cheddar. Jackson tries to sneakily scare him but by the looks of George's face, he isn't fazed.

George says " Ciao bratr, got to try harder to scare me."

Jackson responds asking " Ciao bratr, I will get you! How are you?"

George takes his blue gloves off, after he puts the divided cheddar into separate boxes lined with blue bags, while he does this he responds asking...

" No chance bro, I am feeling good today, payday so I treated myself to a pack of smokes. How are you brother?"

Jackson responds asking " Every payday you do that, anyway I am good bratr, busy today?"

George responds " Yeah bro I work for it otherwise just paying the bills mate, got to treat yourself. Usual Friday lunch bratr."

Jackson responds asking " I second that bro got to treat yourself, quick break?"

George responds saying " Of course bro, one minute."

George goes to the pizza section where the different day labels are kept on the wall, he rips two Monday labels off, taking the blue Barkley's Bank pen from from behind his ear, writing the date on them, after peeling them to put each one on the divided cheddar.

A similar beginning to the next morning, weather wise as it begins. The only difference is that George is standing at a bus stop, not far from his home. Also along with the obvious that is, he has changed his clothes. An elderly lady with a walking stick stands not far away waiting for the same bus, I would presume. There are houses all around opposite the bus stop through the middle like an island is a long green, with trees dotted up it that used to act as goal posts, for when George used to play footie growing up with his brother, but you have to be careful where or how you shoot the football because there are parked cars all along its left side, didn' t want to smash a car window, have to run back indoors then hope the person wouldn' t come knocking at the door, wouldn' t of mattered to George' s pocket money if mum had to pay for the smashed car window, as he didn' t get any, parents not made of money, made him appreciate what he earns, also he smashed a window when he was younger playing with a golf ball, when he stayed at his dads which was situated down a cul de sac, smashed through some mans front door.

A bus comes around the corner followed by a dark blue saloon car, as the bus pulls into the lay-by to pick up its first passengers for this trip around. The bus doors open, George lets the elderly lady go first, the blue car pulls around the bus, George puts his thumb up in the air towards the people, in the blue car because they are his next door neighbors. The elder lady walking deeper into the bus to find a seat while George hops on to the bus.

He asks the bus driver " Yo bud, can I have a day rider please?"

The bus driver responds saying " Certainly, four pound fifty please."

George passes him a fiver from his jean pocket, passing it too him through the hole in the glass, to protect us from the violent bus drivers, of course I'm joking apart from the road rage they may encounter because of other idiots on the road. The bus driver fiddles around on the ticket machine for a second, a ticket printed out from the machine that George takes, after takes his fifty pence piece change.

George says " Cheers."

He goes deeper into the bus to find a seat at the back.

The bus arrives into the towns city center, more people have ascended into the bus during its journey.

It stops at the second bus stop in, of the four bus stops. Different cultures waiting to get onto the bus, George grabs ahold of his backpack putting it on, where it belongs. He walks down the walkway of the bus, joining the line of different people getting off, still some people are sitting down, that elderly lady that got on with George got off three stops back, while getting off to the bus driver.

George says " Thank you. "

George puts into his left ear a earphone, after fiddling around on his mobile for a second, a favorite song starts to play from the left. He starts walking through the town towards his place of work, as he puts the right earphone in. Walking past a bank while feeling the vibe of the rapper in his ear. A guy in raggedy tattered clothes begging at the side of the street, more people around this morning. Across the road is Christ college, you can really see the beautiful collection of architectural buildings, the attention to detail is incredible of these colleges also churches in my city of Cambridge.

As George is walking to his place of work, David2Marseille, he lights his smoke after puts the lighter back in his pocket. Some broken glass on the floor from a smashed bottle, most probably from a messy night, most probably the cause of George's flat tire, two open cans of some branded alcohol in front of the wall that George is walking past, I am sure the walking homeless, will scoop them up before the council put them in the bin or anyone for that matter, not even George, just walking past them They would have to sniff them before consumption, just incase it's piss. I'm not judging them I personally wouldn't do it but live your movie mate.

Jackson is sitting on the restaurants step, the same age as George twenty four. They sideway bump fists after George takes a cigarette from behind his ear, he lights it while Jackson stands up, three bins at the side while Jackson rolls a cigarette with a filter.

Jackson says asking " Bro what happened? I see you walking up here, not biking?"

George responds asking " Flat tire bro, how are you?"

Jackson dressed in casual clothes responds saying " I am alright, yourself?"

George watching passers-by while passing Jackson his lighter.

He responds asking " Not too bad bro, can't wait for my day off tomorrow."

Jackson responds saying " Oh right, I hope you have a nice day, I have Monday off."

George asks " You up to much?"

Jackson responds asking " Treat my lady to some dinner then cinema, you bro?"

George responds asking " Yeah bro, seeing my little lady, going to pick her up from her mum's, park then a bite to eat, she likes to make her own Sub, her way."

A black six-seater taxi pulls up...

Carlo the pasta chef alongside the Romanian kitchen porter called Cezar. They all smack their hands together bumping shoulders, while the black taxi door slides open, the assistant manager, Aida gets out from the back.

She says in her thick French accent, " Sorry guys for being late, I had a early morning of drinking. "

The chefs take ahold of the bins, while she walks up to the restaurant doors with keys in her hand, to unlock the white doors. Carlo is from Brazil, he has short styled brown hair, dark brown eyes, a few tattoos of loved ones on his arms, also a tattoo of a wolf on his left upper arm, he is wearing shades with a black vest top, grey tracks bottoms. Five o' clock shadow, good geezer but when pissed off turns into a real life pissed off wolf mate, I would like him on my side if shit kicks off.

Old school garage music playing from the portable speaker. George along with the other chefs are dressed in all black chef uniform, the time is 11:37am Prep for lunch is nearly finished, there is pasta in a massive sieve, that is in a big silver saucepan. Aida puts a tray with coffees on down on top of a silver top chest freezer. Her anchor tattoo showing either side of her black dresses strap, that is on her left shoulder. Her shoulder length dark blonde hair, blue eyes, she has a curvy figure. Jackson picks up an expresso from the black tray,

while saying " Smoke break before the place opens. "

George says " I will second that brother. "

They are standing outside the kitchen door, George is putting three cubes sugars in his coffee, stirring with a long silver spoon, he stirs his coffee while the other three chefs are sitting in a booth, with red leather seats, they are rolling cigarettes.

Amelia, a waitress is walking towards them, a beautiful petite figure with bushy ginger hair, light green eyes, she is wearing jeans with a Liverpool football team shirt, that is where the rest of her family is, she is young with cute facial features.

She says " Morning all."

She puts her bag down on the table after Amelia hugs George. They all go for a cigarette apart from Amelia because in her spare time she does ballet so she doesn' t smoke.

The same style of music is playing, it is halfway through a busy service, restaurant is nearly full, on the pass is a seafood risotto, lamb burger with a pepperoni pizza, that a Italian waiter, Anthony an muscle head pretty boy, with slicked black hair, is taking the food from the kitchen to the customers. George puts down a basket of fries in the scolding hot oil of the fryer. After he turns a burger with a spatula, with yellow tongs he takes a double breasted chicken, from the grill placing it on to a black tray, after brushes oil mixed with salt, pepper also parsley over the chicken, he puts the tray into the bottom pizza oven.

Jackson says " Carlo, Two minutes for table six!"

Carlo puts his thumb up from across the kitchen.

George says asking " Bro five for table seven alongside fourteen!?"

Jackson responds saying " Yes bratr!"

George is preparing plates for the upcoming tickets, he has a line of tickets, the ticket machine sounds while it prints another one out, George puts a pot of relish down on a paper lined tray. He takes the ticket, his eyes scanning over, he passes it to the kitchen porter because it's a dessert ticket, Jackson his back to George which is alongside Carlo, that is putting a teaspoon of garlic, in a scorching oiled pasta pan, after adding the same amount of diced Chili's in oil to the pan, it sizzles away, while the flames flicker up the pans sides. Jackson is filling a calzone, with some Cajun spiced chicken, the calzone was my favorite pizza to make, I perfected them, but being on the pizza section is fucking hard mate, I went on it a couple of times on Saturdays, I can happily say I failed more than a couple of times, there is a art to it, although I can make a pizza but under that pressure is mad, because you are basically in charge of everything in the kitchen while maintaining quality of food, which I can do until I start running out of shit, it's never a quick thing to prep then quickly get back into the flow of service, then run out of another thing, oh man. That's why Jackson also his brother usually work on the pizza section, also that's why their so skinny.

The end of the night is on for the restaurant staff, not much of a busy day. The head chef along with Andrej has joined them for the evening shift. It is ten o'clock. The manager Chris went home an hour ago, but the assistant manager is still here in the office, Amelia along with Anthony are cleaning the restaurants table also bar, every so often bringing in things to be washed. Also the Hungarian bar man that is cleaning the glasses, he is a big geezer, really short hair, brown eyes. The waiters also waitresses wear black jeans or trousers with a black company t' shirt, also a green waiters apron, that they put their white ordering pads also pens, inside the pouch at the front like a kangaroo that keeps her young.

It's eleven o'clock the kitchen along with restaurant is clean. The kitchen staff along with waiting staff are having a drink at the bar before they go home, George drinking Jackie D whiskey mixed with coke, the ladies drinking white wine while the others are drinking beer from bottles. Everyone is in there normal everyday clothes. Anthony flexing in the mirrors that are in rustic frames all over the restaurant wall.

He asks " Who is up for going out to a night clubs?"

Before anyone can respond, a figure at the restaurants doors catches their attention, his face pressed up against the glass.

George says " If this guy fall down there, going to sleep because he is too pissed, I will break his legs to get out."

Amelia says " Maybe he has been in a fight."

Carlo says " Looks like he lost."

Leaving blood on the window in the shape of his face, smearing downwards.

The guy eventually comes in, dressed in a white blood covered shirt, black trousers with his wet blood soaked dark blue tie wrapped around his right hand, because his hand is squeezed tightly, droplets of blood leaving the tie splashing below. He doesn't have whites to his eyes they are just dark red. He is groaning while his jaw snapping together like a vicious dog, his hands grabbing at the moment fin air, his left cheek starts to peel away from his face, splattering on the wooden floor, teeth alongside gumstarts falling fromthe hollowed cheek.

Everyone starts to panic while asking the same question "What the fuck!?"

George grabs both of the women putting thembehind the men while they back away, throwing anything in sight at the rotting man.

Aida throws a wine glass that smashes off his head, Anthony throws a brown handles steak knife that pierces through the other cheek, but doesn't stay in his mouth, for too long because that side peels away fromhis face, clattering alongside splattering to the wooden ground, like a ships decking. Amelia throws a couple menus at him doesn't even give him a paper cut.

Jackson cracks a joke "We just sold out of our human brain sir."

George says " I have a idea, I will come back."

George runs into the kitchen.

He comes back with a red handled knife, walking up the guy that grabs ahold of George's jacket, bringing himcloser.

George uppercut stabs the guy while saying " Man your breath be stinking, ever heard of a mint, Christ almighty."

The guy releasing George that swipes the knife out of his head, as his eyes go black like a laptop shutting down, as he crumbles to the ground, laying on top of the menus.

Jackson tells Aida " You have keys in your bag, so you can lock the fucking door, so we can figure out what this shit is."

She starts rummaging through her black handbag. George takes a chair putting it under the handle of the door, digging it into the square rug.

While telling whoever will listen " Can you dim the lights? so we can see better outside, there could be more. "

Amelia dims the lights, everyone staying low while looking outside, a bus stop opposite the restaurant, to their right you can see the beginning of the road bridge, that goes over the river Cam

Whispering the head chef says " We need weapons. "

George pulls out his cigarettes, lighting one up.

Aida asks " What you doing? You can' t smoke in here. "

George says " Well you don' t think I am going out there to smoke. "

Cezar says " It is not that bad. "

Andrej responds " It might be, look. "

He points in to the dark of the night, a figure kneeling on the floor munching the contents of someone else' s stomach. George watching Aida' s face wince in terror at watching this he offers her a cigarette, in which she takes him up on the offer.

George saying " Well At least there won' t be no vomit on the streets tomorrow, the crows will have to find another meal. "

Jackson responds saying " Just some humans flesh to peck at. "

George says " Well when one door shuts another opens. "

Aida lights up the cigarette, while shaking a little.

George still bending down at the front window, smoking. He says, " We are going to need resources, weapons, we could be the only people left or we need to find help at least."

Carlo swigging on his beer responds saying " It is true, we need to get some weapons also stuff to protect this place because it could be our fortress for a while."

George asks " Who wants to check the street situation out with me?"

Amelia, Carlo along with the Hungarian man Adam, put their hands up. The head chef is sitting at one of the tables, rolling a big cigarette, a grinder beside.

George says " Save me some."

They go back into the kitchen to get protection if needed for everyone. While they go there a police car comes streaming down with their light flashing, but hits something in the road, that causes it to flip.

George drags the dead Z out from restaurant, droplets of blood from the Zs wounds smearing as he is dragged from the wooden floor onto the square welcome rug carpet, past that onto the cold concrete street floor, sitting his slumped body against the wall beside the entrance, while Carlo, Adam alongside Amelia step out from the restaurant onto the street, the glow to their right is coming from the crashed flipped police car, light flickering on the figure beside the fire, on all fours eating the contents of someone' s stomach. They start to walk left towards, Sains____s. They are going there for resources. The streets ahead look too quiet apart from hearing commotion, Adam alongside Carlo agree to cross the street, to cover both sides, all armed with a kitchen knife. George alongside Amelia crouching while walking to try not to be detected. All the lights in Café Red are off, the place looks dead apart from the glow behind them from the flaming paddy wagon. They carry on stealthily walking past another French restaurant, shards of glass on the path, from a hole in the window that is apart of the wall, that has a table half hanging out. The restaurant has erupted into chaos as the different customer eating the front of house staff instead of what the chefs have made. They are stepping over the broken glass.

While George whispers " I never understood why this restaurant is always full, Polish kitchen staff, Italian waiting staff making French food. "

Amelia responds saying " I know, I wanted to work here but they turned me down, the tips are amazing. "

Inside of the restaurant a Z is eating the stomach contents of a darker haired male waiter, lungs along with intestines spilling out, a group of five chefs walk out from the kitchen, armed with knives, droplets of blood drying on their whites, the front chef is a hefty geezer, rolled up sleeves to reveal colorful tattoos, armed with a meat cleaver, a Z running towards him with jaw snapping. *Whack!* meat cleaver sticking out from the falling Z. Carlo alongside Adam walking further up, George beside Amelia crossing over a turning onto a side road. Another window from the restaurant explodes outwards followed by the cause a chair. A shiny black motorbike is approaching towards, the person riding bent forward, a person on the back arms around the drivers waist, the visor open. George sees the blood eyes of the woman on the back, that takes her helmet off lobbing it behind her, rolling along the tarmac, as they speed past. The pair of them walking past a small church that's beside a pub, the motorbike hits into the fire engulfed police car, explosions over their shoulder.

All four arrive at the orange chain supermarket, all the Z's must have heard the surrounding clubs music, gone there to feed on the living. A body laying further up on the cobble road, chained together orange deep trolleys, a pound coin to free one.

George says " Stay alert guys, cover each others backs, get things that will help us if we have to hold up in the restaurant for a few days."

Carlo says " This reminds me of Brazil, man I left there because I was afraid of someone ending my life."

Adam says " Same man but mine was more for a job also money, but there is faszfejek everywhere bro."

Amelia loudly whispers " Wait up George!"

They walk into the shop after him

Products are all over grey laminated floor, a cheese counter is beside them as they carry on walking towards the rows of tills. A shopping trolley with a box of sanitary towels lay on the bottom A dead chunky female workers slumped over the first till, in the middle a male with a darker skin complexion, laying over the tills conveyer belt. They stand beside the veg along with fruit isle with a meat fridge to start the isle, backing onto a tinned isle. George walks over to the till, the register is open on the first one, he starts taking the five, ten, twenty along with all of the fifty pound notes out, stashing them in his pocket, with the one also two pound coins.

Amelia asks " What are you doing? We need to get food not money."

George responds saying " Yes we will but being a chef in a chain restaurant don't pay that well, eventually this will end, while I am doing this, take that trolley, fill it up with food also drink, alcohol as well."

Carlo is pointing beside George that looks, to see the cashier, sitting upright, her eyes red with chucks of her chubby cheeks falling down her into her lap, her teeth grinding together with each snap like someone that is pilled up.

George jumping while shouting " Oh Shit!"

His red handled knife stabbing through the middle of her forehead, skull cracking through the other side, while she slumps forward, blood trickling down the back of her neck, her hair being in a ponytail like well a ponies tail. George removes his knife while some of her brittle skin is stuck to his blade, he grabs to wipe, with a carrier bag moving onto the next till.

Adam laughing while smacking Carlo's back saying " She looked like a shit unicorn."

George joins in with laughing, while stuffing his pockets, but Amelia doesn't share the same humor.

The other two go to find to fill a trolleys while Adam stays with George that is moving around the tills filling his pockets with cash from the tills, occasionally having to kill an undead cashier. While Adam has found a basket to fill with meat.

George alongside Adam are walking with a full basket each, George's filled with cigarettes also tobacco along with papers also lighters. They turn walking down isle seven, a customer services mans body lay in a puddle of blood, a basket tipped over its contents spilled, a plastic wrapper of a knife lay on the ground but no sight of the weapon.

George says " Someone didn't like the customer service here."

Adam says " Check out this killer deal, you buy one, get one free."

Both stepping over his lifeless legs to find the other two.

They find them down the alcohol isle, half filled trolley with different types of tinned food. They start taking bottles from the shelves, George goes straight for the whiskey alongside dark rum as the others are putting bottles of vodka along with other spirits inside.

George asks " Did you get mixers?"

Amelie says " No, we was going to get them next."

George nods his head, while Adam takes two dark squares bottles from him putting in the trolley.

He responds saying " Okay I will go find them, join me when your done here."

George walks off to do what he just said.

George walks down the isle, past shelves of wine, around a few bottles of red that are smashed on the ground. Droplets of red wine dripping from the pointy broken bottle joining the puddle. He looks both ways still not another life full soul insight, just empty checkouts apart from the middle one. He turns right past promotional shelves to the last isle in the shop, his eyes scanning each shelf, he sees the lemonade bottles in the middle. Opposite white double doors, George is walking to the middle of the isle.

He shouts " They are the next isle guys!"

Carlo shouts " Alright bro, be there in a second!"

George starts grabbing off from the middle shelf boxes of twenty-four coke cans.

A muscular mixed race man, he looks like he takes care of his physical appearance, dressed in black trousers also a scruffy white shirt, blood dripping from his bottom lip, some droplets splattering on the ground or joining the others on his shirt, twisted name badge ' Jerry' in white on a orange background, underneath is ' Store Supervisor' pushing the door behind George open.

George turns his head, nodding up asking " Yo bro, you want to give me a hand?"

He turns his head back grabbing ahold of the red box. Jerry' s hand grabs ahold of George' s shoulder.

That says " Nah mate not today, I am not food."

George smashes the red coke can box over Jerry' s head, on impact cans start tearing through the cardboard, as he hits again, red cans flying through the air. Before they hit the floor, George pops Jerry in the nose. The others hearing the commotion start coming around, especially when the cans hit the floor, spinning off with coke squirting out. Jerry' s teeth falling from his mouth every time they rapidly close together, like a dog that has fucking rabies. Jerry not even dazed by being punched along with a box filled with cans over his head, starts going towards George with his hands out in a strangling stance, George starts to panic but not wanting to die, he hooks the Z in the side of its head, on impact Adams yellow handled chefs knife that is usually used for cooked meat, but instead is flying through the air, George's closed fist indenting more of Jerry's face that's stumbling back, while the knives tip pierces through the ear drum on the other side. The Z's body is quick to start falling to the floor, George's fist pulls away along with some black haired skin from the Z's beard. As the body thumps the ground, the plastic handle connecting with the laminated flooring.

George says " Thanks brother, nice shot!"

Adam stands with Carlo, Amelia eventually joins them with the trolley.

Adam says " I was brought up with knives because I lived on a farm in my country, Hungary also I see your knife on the shelf."

George picks up sealed red can, cracking it open to drink. George along with Amelia go to find anything that will help with barricading, while the other two carry on collecting more food, moving onto the biscuit along with crisps.

Back at the restaurant, the others are still locked inside, the head chef, with his younger brother also Andrej are smoking at a table, while the others are keeping look out for the other four to arrive back.

Aida says " It can't be all that bad, buses are still running."

The bus starts swerving, seeing the bus driver hands swaying side to side, as he is gripping tighter to the steering wheel, while a female Z is chomping on his neck.

The bus goes past with the buses logo 'Citi.' which is white in a red circular shape. blue, orange alongside white on the side of the double decker. An advertisement in the middle of the decks, of a book also cinema screenings, which is what I want. That has just recently come out called' An Essence Of Time" so go get that please! keep supporting. Driving past on both decks people from different cultures also genders eating each other. Until it looses control, clipping the burning cop car, flipping over.

In the club, Vodka Revs is becoming over run by Z's. Loud music playing any survivors are behind the bar, broken bottles at the ready, jabbing or slicing at any Z that gets close enough. Shards of beer bottles over the counter, a row of people with black t' shirts on, with the clubs logo on the front in the middle, along with a young lady with a silver sparkling pencil dress also a smartly dressed chap with a stylish blue shirt on. His name is Shane, he whacks a second bottle on the bar counter, beer along with glass splash everywhere, he is standing next to the not so camouflaged sparkly dressed girl.

He says asking " My name is Shane, what's yours?"

She responds saying " My name is Summer."

Shane responds saying " You are certainly bright like a summers day."

She is forced to stab a man Z in the face with a broken bottle, Shane forcibly pushes in a broken beer bottle in to another Z's eye, across the bar, that is quick to go into the back of his rotting skull.

Another mans voice shouts over all the noise" Follow me to the back door!!"

Five young bar people rushing, the other two following them to a door that leads out to the back. As a guy on the dance floor that would have been grinding between this lady's booty, that is wearing a dark blue pencil skirt, it's a bit of waste, because she has nice legs with cute facial features, the guy taking chunks out of the lady neck, someone should tell him they prefer to be kissed, blood spilling changing the blue to red, his arms wrapped around her waist. Got to show love to these musicians Devlin ft Giggs ' Shot Music.' "Call it murder on the dance floor." Blaring through the speakers as the DJ is too busy chomping on females fingers, now that's finger chomping good.

Packs of different drinks stacked up in the warehouse, a guy with short black hair, forces the door shut from the Z's that are trying to get in, severing one of their Z hands in the process, that flops to the ground. Shane helps by barging into the door, while the others block up the door with stuff that is laying around. His name badge on ' John' in red on a black background, dark brown styled slicked back hair with tattoos all over his arms. Pulling a shelving unit full of cases of beer across to block the door while another woman that works there, with a name badge on saying ' Trainee.' Petite in build with tied up shiny black hair, pulls a yellow bulky floor cleaning machine out from a side room to block the door. While the others check if the back door exit is clear.

A mans voice shouts through to them " Come on guys, get a fucking move on, it is clear!"

The three run to join them after blocking the door, shutting the back door on their way out.

Further up on every outskirts of the town center, the armed police, to contain the situation have set up road blocks, so the Z virus doesn' t overspill to the unaware people, that are in their homes. But the people that are on their survival missions inside the city center doesn' t know this. It is already lam just got to make it to the morning, the army is on their way, as no other city has a Z problem Every copper has been pulled in to cover so every way that the Z' s can go through to the neighborhoods has at least two coppers, posted at with machine guns, only allowing survivors to pass through.

Back to George, that has ahold of Adam' s knife, he cleaned it on the supervisors shirt, Amelia walking beside him with a green handled knife in one hand, in her other hand a red handled one. Carlo at the front of the trolley lifting it up, while Adam is the opposite side lifting the trolley up, otherwise it would make a racket if they was pushing it on the cobble road. One side is a wall to a university, in the background. On the other side is a sports shop next to that is a DVD along with book selling shop, that is beside a barbers. They walk altogether, while George keeps a look out behind them

They walk further up, still not a sign of anyone dead or alive.

Adam says " Let's stop for a minute, I workout but my arms will hurt in the morning."

They put the trolley down in the middle of the road, a family pack of Waller crisps falls off from the trolley, Amelia nearly jumps out of her fucking skin mate, thinking a Z is behind her, George chuckles while he picks the crisps up, putting them back on the trolley.

While Carlo says " Yeah should of brought Tony with us, he would of lifted this fucker by himself."

George says " Yeah, that's why Amelia likes him, we shouldn't talk about her B F like that."

Carlo says " She must like being lifted up."

Amelia protest " He isn't my boyfriend actually guys."

George chuckles " That's what they all say up until five minutes before they start to play tonsil tennis, he isn't the only one who can lift you up."

Adam pipes in saying " Or throw you around the bedroom"

George fist bumps Adam in agreement as Amelia blushes a little.

Carlo says " We are only joking Amelia, he is only interested in easy girls, not classy."

George scoffs while responding " Classy, not an ounce she supports Liverpool."

Adam this time fist bumps George in agreement, while Amelia smacks George's arms, sticking her tongue out at George, which does it back.

On the corner of the road, behind them is a sweet shop, across the road in front of them is a gravel driveway that leads to a university, that has such beautiful architecture even the most hardened gangster, would appreciate the beauty of the building. Across the road from the university is the beginning of the restaurants starting with a burger chain. On both sides of the road is a black bollard, but they have stopped before that on a zebra crossing that links the round church to the sweet shop, which used to be a cigar shop. A ice cream stand, lays smashed on the floor the same side as the university. George walks over to the ice cream stand, looking down the road, seeing a silver car wrapped around a lamppost, the car doors open with the car alarm has slowly starts to breakdown.

George asks " Carlo bro, you scoop ice cream on the side, in your spare time?"

Carlo responds saying " I know bro, it has my name on the side, I have tried tasted ice cream from it as well, not bad to be honest bro."

George looks over, tubs of ice cream laying over the pavement, a Z on all fours eating a severed arm, biting off a thumb, blood smeared around his chops. George starts backing away, he turns his head while putting his index finger to his lips.

Amelia mouths asking " Is there one?"

George nods, a woman' s screams breaks through the silent of the night.

The Z looks up while his teeth are munching trough the thumb flesh to bone. He puts the arm down after grabs ahold of a pink tub of lidless ice cream, it has started to defrost by the looks, it has chunks of red strawberry mixed in. The Z stands up after scoops his hand in, pulling out ice cream, his hand like a bowl, as he lifts it to his mouth, spilling over the edges, he does this again until the tub is finished, half on the floor, as he swallows the ice cream, he drops the tub to the pavement. Melting ice cream dripping from the fingers of the Z, that pushes his palm in to the front of his head while stomping up then down, by the looks of it brain freeze has kicked in. George chuckles out load! which the Z hears, skin comes away with his palm, stuck to his forehead. The Z roars towards him after starts climbing over the ice cream stand, George is backing up towards the other three, he reaches his hand back for Amelia to pass him a weapon. At the same time as the Z starts running towards George, his hand clutched ahold of a bottles neck, he swings with all his power. Slowing it down for you to see the impact on the left side of the Z's jaw, nearly spinning the Z's head around then around again, blood, ice cream, teeth, chunks of strawberries along with flesh spray in all directions. Cracks form in the bottles dark glass, they spread up the bottle like roots, pieces of glass burst out with the white wine following. Back to normal time, the whole bottle shatters shards exploding everywhere as the Z falling with his jaw still swinging.

Carlo says " The spirit of Jesus was in that swing!"

George drops the chunks of glass in his hand to the concrete pavement. The others look on shocked while George takes a hold of one of the baskets from the trolley.

He says " Come on, you want to be there next meal."

They all start walking back to the restaurant.

They arrive back at the restaurant, while Carlo
at one end, Adam at the other are taking the trolley
through the restaurants doorway. Amelia is already
inside getting a drink, something that is stronger
than a coffee. George is keeping lookout, he looks
down the way that they come, his eyes scanning around
only seeing bits of destruction, such as restaurant
also pub windows smashes outwards, a silver taxi that
crashed into bike rails. He looks the other way,
towards the bridge that goes over the river cam, a
exploded upside down cop car at the mouth of the
bridge. He notices the bus from earlier but he
didn' t see flipped to crashed into the other
vehicles causing a blockade, nothing is getting
through the flaming pile, so they are safer on one
side, but he can' t see Z' s or anyone alive for that
matter, just burning corpses. George walks into the
restaurant while getting a cigarette out to smoke.

Still inside the center of town, in a clubs open
roof, a stocky bald headed bouncer with a bushy
chestnut brown beard, is hiding behind a bar with a
young lady in a blue glittery dress. He peeps over
the top of the bar counter, there is a group of seven
Z' s on the dance floor, every so often they keep
bumping into each other, snarling at one another like
a pack a rabies bitten dogs. Retro sofas around the
edges of the room with retro coffee tables in the
middle, stopping at the closed door that is to the
side of the bar, one bit of noise will alert the Zs.
He grabs a hold of a silver cork screw. She grabs a
small serrated brown handled knife, from a wooden
chopping board, that would have been used for slicing
or wedging lemon along with limes.

Back into the restaurant, George is pouring a glass of whiskey mixed with coke after putting the money he collected at the supermarket in his backpack. He takes his glass from the bar counter.

Adam says " Bro I am going to have the same as you. "

George is walking over to a seat, his phone sits face down on the table.

George responds saying " Knock yourself out bro. "

He sits down, swirling around the jack to mix with the coke, taking a swig after putting his glass down, picking his phone up he starts to text, while the ladies are keeping watch outside, the others are sorting through the trolleys.

George stands up putting his mobile in his pocket he finishes off his drink. He notices two people stealth walking on the other side of the street.

George asks " Girls, you see them two as well?"

Aida responds saying " Yes I do, they are not looking Z to me. "

George goes to take the chair that is stuffed under the handle also into the doormat, unbolting the door, poking his head out.

George loudly whispers " Pssssst! Over here!"

They both stop in their tracks at the bus stop, after realizing that it's not a flesh eating Z, that is calling them over for its next meal. The guy has something in his hand, talking to each other while they're crossing the road to George. When an elderly Z geezer, swerving across the road towards the two of them on a red motorized scooter.

George shouts " Watch out!"

Wham! Shane takes the Z off from the scooter with his brown hockey stick.

While he is smashing the Z's head in with the hockey stick, blood spurting upwards with every hit.

He says " These things are starting to piss me off!"

The young woman that he is with, drags him away from the Z, into the restaurant away from any other Z's that could have been alerted.

While Tony behind the bar is pouring a drink for Shane alongside Summer, which have just introduced themselves. In front of them is George offering them a cigarette, Amelia also Aida is standing either side of George, Adam sitting on a chair beside, cleaning his yellow handle knife. The other's push the trolley, wheeling to store in the kitchen while Carlo sits guarding the back of the restaurant. They both take a smoke, the same as George takes one out, putting it between his lips, lighting his then theirs, don't worry Aida has already disarmed the fire alarm, otherwise they would have been overrun by now, it would be to the Z's what a cop siren is to a robber, in that scenario they would be the thief, get the fuck out of there, quickly, because the single plane glass wouldn't be much protection.

George asks " What happened?"

He lights his cigarette after lights theirs while Tony hands them their drinks, while Shane explains.

Going into a cut scene, Shane is narrating while your watching the events unfold. We was with five others who worked behind the bar of the night club we was in, now only us two are left, the whole dance floor turned to flesh eating pricks quickly, people instead of dancing, drinking, touching to kissing, you know enjoying a night out on the town, it turnt to eating one another, only god know the cause. Anyway from having a piss in the toilets turned around to see the toilet attendant getting eaten, thank my LuckY stars for deodoraN mate, had to burn my eX as well, enjoyed that, set a couple of other people on fire on my way down them stairs, fuck right off if I am getting eaten, I managed to make it to behind the bar where I met Summer along with the others.

We got to the back door escaping out of the Z filled night club, for a split second I even believed we was all safe. We made it to an alley way behind the club, there was a lot more Zs waiting for us. Blocking both exits to the towns streets, also tight squeezes in the alley because of the big fuck-off bins, you know the red ones with the black lids. There is three of them in a row, cigarette butts lay heavily on the ground mixed with a couple of condom packets also a half filled condoms poorly stuffed in the bins, already spewed out, in a pile of the ground. (You can almost hear any woman go " That' s disgusting." Even know they are the cause, especially if their tight. Someone kicked a empty beer bottle which alerts the Zs, they come running from both sides towards us, the bar people try fighting off the Zs but failing, shit I see a Z bite a chunk out of this fella' s neck. So I jumped onto one of the bins, felt a tug at my ankle. Looked back to see Summer I helped her up, we ran like hell over the bins, that is fucking hard by the way, doesn' t help when Zs trying to grab your legs, anyway then we ran out of the alley way, I don't think a single soul survived, most probably still in the alley.

We was walking down the middle of the road, the supermarket coming up on our left, a person laying face down, in front of the store. I could see a group of people ahead of us, with a trolley. We was walking towards them folks. Well that person that was on the ground had gotten up, he grabbed ahold of me, which made both of us jump but Summer screamed, I swear on that. He then flung me into the sports shop front door that swung open on my impact, I fell onto the ground, Summer ran in there after me to help me up before the Z could. I quickly grabbed ahold of the nearest thing I could, which was this hockey stick. We could hear moaning also rustling behind us so we got out of that shop as fast as possible. I quickly beat the dead out of the Z, which was just in front of the door, that Summer closed, now we are here standing in front of you guys, oh yeah we see the Z with a swung around head.

Back to the restaurant George is standing while smoking a cigarette.
He says " Oh right, well you guys can defiantly stay with us."
Summer says " I really appreciate that."
Aida along with Amelia are quick to take her under their wing, as they help clean up her, makeup smeared all over her show, while Adam is keeping lookout.
Shane shakes George's hand while saying " Same, it is appreciated bro."
George stubs out his cigarette after taking his last drag.

George says " There could be more survivors out there, we need to go back down there."

Adam says " Yeah I will come, beats waiting here."

Shane says " You got my attention, I am in."

Tony says " Yes bro, I am on that."

George says " Alright bro, go get Carlo to stay down here with the women, even though they are safer with the Z' s.

Tony chuckles after nods after goes down the corridor to the others, George makes himself a drink.

While saying " Lads get something to eat, drink, smoke because it will be five minutes before we go, I need to drop the kids off at the swimming pool, I am starting to turtle head."

Amelia chuckles while saying " You' re grim"

George puts his drink down while quickly shuddering in a state of panic towards the toilets.

while he responds saying " That maybe, but I am truthful."

George while muttering " I don' t think I can make it, I will have to use the disabled ones."

He turns the corner, while Adam gets up to go get a drink as Shane is watching the outside, eyes scanning everywhere to spot any flickering of movements.

Back to the bouncer alongside the young girl, that nearly brakes her ankle because of her shiny heels. They are walking down the street, broken glass all over the place, they come down to the bottom of one road to a t-junction, a wall is in front of them

Tracy says " I am going to need some proper shoes because these heels are killing me off."

Bobby the bouncer says " Lets get you some, we will go Grafton."

They turn left away from the armed police road block, they don' t know it is there, which would have been their safest bet to survive. Lifeless bodies lay everywhere, some are smartly dressed others wearing casual clothes. A homeless couple lay in their sleeping bags in a closed shop entrance, they look like they are sleeping but could also be dead. Devastation has wrecked the streets above, bus shelters smashed, rubbish everywhere, taxis are burning with crispy corpses inside, even in the number one bus all the lights are off, doors look shut but the bus driver didn' t get far, I hear you ask how do I know, he didn' t get far? Because he lays beside a black public bin being eaten.

Tracy says " Fuck going down there, we are certainly not making it through to the other side alive, you know some of them fuck nugget Zs are just laying there sleeping, one slight noise they going to be on our tails."

Before Bobby can respond Tracy' s left heel snaps, he decides to sweep her off her feet so she doesn' t damage her feet, putting her over his right shoulder, she throws her heel less shoe on the ground.

Bobby says " Watch my back, we will go a different way."

Tracy stretches back grabbing her other heel off, Bobby puts his cork screw between the marriage alongside middle fingers on his left hand.

Tracy says " If they get too close, I will stab them with my heel or this knife."

Bobby responds saying " That would be appreciated. "

They are walking past a bank that leads to a poorly lit alley way that runs through behind the bus depot.

Back at the armed police, that is holding up a part of the outskirts, *Short burst of gun fire.* They are holding off one of the longest roads, also busiest parts of town because it has rows of restaurants along with the clubs. Two police cars with four armed police stand, they have all four streets covered. All four are dressed in full bodied black armed police uniform from the helmet to the boots, they are most probably wearing armed police underwear with socks. Each have a assault rifle, the G36 along with a Glock 17 in a holster around their legs. There is also two HK417 one is in left cop cars, each of the cop cars blocking the four roads. A paddy wagon drives from behind them, parking up beside the The church of Our lady also the English Martyrs. A police officer gets out walking over to a armed officer that is on one knee, with the other HK417, that is set up on the bonnet of his cop car, silencer attached, his G36 resting on the floor to his right.

The police officer stands beside the armed officer saying, " The streets look clear from Zs, just drunken teenagers, considering it is two in the morning. "

The armed officer says " Good, can' t let this problem overspill, all we have to do is hold this position until the morning. "

A helicopter is flying over behind with a bright spotlight on, sweeping all of the outskirts.

The police officer that has a stab proofed vest on says," I am going to check out the infected zone, there could be survivors."

Before anyone can say another word, the armed officer starts shooting. Looking down the scope to one outer circle, to a smaller middle circle, to a dot in the middle, that is moving from bloodied shirt torso to face of the approaching Z. Trying not to wake any of the other Zs, that is where the silencer comes in handy, even though there is still gun fire coming from the others. A bullet rips through the approaching Zs head, moving to another Z, until the police officer takes the pistol from the armed officers leg holster, after puts a bullet through the Zs eyes, blood along with brain explodes out back onto a draping white table cloth, as it was climbing out of a Chinese restaurants smashed out window frame, but is now slumped over the windows wooden frame.

George is walking down the street with the other three, they are checking in windows also down the street, in parked cars for anyone that isn't a Z yet. They come across the occasional body on the ground or seat, that is when they check to see if there is life, the Z in them comes out, they have to quickly kill them

George says " We should go to the sports shop first, we can get more weapons."

They all agree while they carry on walking down the street towards the sports shop.

Tony with his Italian accent saying " This is all we need."

Flakes of snow start heavily falling from the sky.

Shane responds saying" I hope it don' t settle or carry on for too long, our vision will be buggered mate."

They all stop at the sports shop, George opens the door to the eerie dark building.

All four of them enter the sports shop, outlines of rackets on the wall, with football t' shirts on clothes rails, football, cricket, tennis equipment are on display stands throughout the store.

George asks " Anyone bring a flashlight?"

Adam pulls his phone out, fiddling around for a sec before a beam of light rays out from the back.

Adam whispers " Got to love Aye-phones."

Shane whispers in response" They are the best phone, but I bet they hack into your phones without you knowing, just to spy in your life."

Adams light keeps swaying but no one notices a Z that has flesh hanging out from his mouth, his white blood drenched t' shirt has the companies logo, to tell us he once worked here.

Adam responds in disbelief whispering his question, " No chance they could spy on us, why would they?"

Tony whispers his responds saying, " They are like our parents, always wanting to know what is happening, I wouldn' t be surprised if they caused this outbreak."

Tony is quickly interrupted by Shane that says " Don' t be silly, they want more people on the planet, so they can make more money."

George jumps in saying" I think it was tainted meat, we had a new lamb burger that was popular today, also it being its first full day on sale, now there is Zs. Also why would the government or corporate companies do anything to jeopardize their safety along with money income, yeah they wouldn' t, also I have no idea why your whispering. ''

Before anyone can responds the Z has made his presence be known to the other 3 by grabbing a hold of Tony.

Tony starts fighting with the Z, throwing some punches while avoiding being the 'un-dead' s next meal.

George shouting instruction to Adam " Point that over here bro!"

The ray of light leaves Tony fighting with the Z for a couple of seconds, to aid George, that is taking ahold of a cricket bat as Shane grabs a baseball bat, they both swing at the Z' s head at the same time. *Crunching* on impact the Z falls down to the cold laminated shop floor. Letting go of Tony in the process.

Tony saying " Damn! I am surprised his head didn' t explode, Thanks."

George says " Your welcome bro, you would have done the same."

Shane asks Tony " I don' t get it, how can a man with so many muscles, not be able to fight or throw a hard enough punch to kill a Z."

Tony says " Come on man, they are just for the ladies because it turns them wet to have a man, that looks this good."

George says " Not every lady, maybe the pubescent girls mate, but women want a real man that don' t take longer than them to get ready."

They start taking the bats off from the shelf while George is emptying the till.

Tony responds saying " I don' t mind mate as long as they are older than eighteen. "

Adam fist bumps him while saying " Yeah you know brother. "

Shane asks " What you doing George?"

George while taking clumps of twenty pound notes from the till, putting them in his pocket followed by the ten pound notes, even a couple of fifties, happy days.

He responds saying " Bro, I got shit to pay also Christmas is coming up soon, my daughter isn' t cheap. "

Shane says " I hear that, come on sharing is caring. "

George passes him a bunch of ten along with five pound notes, that he puts in his pocket.

George saying " There you go brother, enjoy. "

Shane says " Cheers bro. "

They carry on looking for weapons.

They step out of the shop, George is wearing a home man united football top over his t' shirt. Adam is wearing a home arsenal top over his, Shane is wearing home man shitty (city) top over his, Tony is wearing a home Chelsea top over his shirt. George has a cricket bat while Shane has a hold of a hockey stick, the other two have ahold of a baseball bat each. George has a full carrier bag also Adam has one as well of football shirts. They carry on walking towards the center of the town. The snow is still falling heavily, every snowflake settling on all the objects below the sky.

George a carrier bag in one with the cricket bat in the other, they walk in the middle of the cobbled road, beside on the left of them is a brick wall that leads to a one of the cities collages. On the right is a travel agent shop, that leads round to a alley way that separates a once popular night club.

George says " Shhh, listen for a second, I swear I can hear footsteps like marching. "

Shane says " Maybe it' s the Army. "

Everyone stops still to listen, faint footsteps also groans are heard. Through the alley way comes three Zs, while another two Zs come running towards them

George alongside Adam drop their carrier bags to be able to defend themselves better. They start fighting with the three Zs. George is hitting one in the head, while Shane goes running towards the other two Zs, jumping through the air, his legs extending sideways, two footing one Z while smacking the other Z on his way through. Both Zs on the floor now clambering over one another to get to Shane, that is trying to get back to his feet. George runs over to help him up, while the other two Z' s, are being dealt with by Adam alongside Tony, batting their heads to a pulp, like using a pestle with mortar.

Meanwhile Bobby with Tracy watching his back are walking towards the Grafton center, public grass either side of the railing. It is a full moon which you can hardly see because of the snow falling from the sky. A lamppost light is flickering behind causing Tracy only to see for a second but sometimes it' s hard for her eyes to adjust between the darkness of the night, to light then darkness, as they walk under a flickering lamppost.

Tracy breaks the silence with, " There looks like a figure approaching. "

Bobby stops with the rows of different types of stores either side of a different pebbled street, a telephone box followed by the many metal black bike racks, bodies lay on the floor but for Bobby not a living soul in sight. For Tracy a different idea, it' s not the living souls to be scared of, just the newly departed ones that are still roaming, well the one that is running towards her, is one to be afraid of. Still armed in her right hand a heel, the other hand a brown handled serrated knife, the Zs face has rotted away, like out of date food it has started to decay. Before the Z can grab ahold of her next meal, the heel is fiercely stabbed into her left eye that pops in its socket, the Z starts flapping around until the heel penetrates through her rotting brain, she falls how Tracy did earlier, legs buckles underneath, as Tracy gets another stab in, through its nostrils with the knife, as she falls to the ground, with the murder weapons still attached like piercings.

Booby asks " Everything alright?"

By this time Tracy' s adrenaline has kicked in, she is breathing heavily from having to kill her first Z.

She responds saying " All good now. "

While he turns around, looking down to witness the death of the Z.

To an old paint-chipping white tower that is situated next to the police station, a police sniper has been placed inside there. A police roadblock with three armed police officers are firing at Zs below. The sniper in the tower is overlooking the large green common, where they hold circuses along with fun fairs throughout the year. The reason why I tell you this is because a winter fair is currently stopped on there for a few weeks, with a big ferris wheel still operating along with the places inside glowing. Illumination, being a attraction for Zs, that most probably went there today or somewhere through the week since it has been perched there since Monday. When they was alive, but now the undead are walking across the field to get there, but none making it because *Gun Shot.* The bullet leaves the barrel of the snipper rifle, like a butler going to serve his master, the bullet speedily flies through the air until impacting with a Zs head.

Bobby while walking with Tracy still slumped over his shoulder are outside the second shop on the left, that is still intact, not smashed window or alarm blaring. A female body lay on the thin layer of snowy ground.

Bobby asks " Just out of curiosity, what size feet are you?"

Tracy says asking " I am a five, why?"

Bobby responds " Because there is a young lady, taking a nap on the ground, she is wearing black pumps that look like your size."

Tracy says " Please say your joking, I am not wearing a dead bitches pumps."

Bobby responds " You will have to, by the looks of it the shop is locked, if we brake the window, it will set the alarm off."

Tracy says " Okay put me down a second, let me look. "

Bobby fetches her forward back on her feet, she stands there shivering a little looking at the female body on the ground.

Tracy says " Okay, they will have to do. "

Bobby bends down, he takes the first shoe off, passing it behind him to Tracy, that puts it on her left foot, before he can take the second one off, the female sits up groaning, so in my opinion under the circumstances, Bobby does the only thing possible, he punched the female Z in the face, knocking her back down, most probably out for the count.

Back to the police sniper in the tower, that is stopping the undead overrunning the wonderland. Headshot dropping another until the sniper scope vision lands on a male Z his face peeling off, chunks of cheek also forehead drop to the muddy ground, until the Z stumbles across a dead body that he starts to eat. The sniper can' t believe his eyes, seeing the flesh on the Zs face, healing with every bit of flesh the undead soul is swallowing.

The sniper grabs his radio off the wooden ledge, asking over it " Sir, did you know if they eat another person their skin regenerates. "

A voice comes back with gun shots in the background " No shit, good to know. "

A bullet explodes out of the snipers barrel, flying through the air, piercing through the middle of the regenerating Z' s face.

George alongside the others with no casualties, just won their battle with the Zs. George lighting a cigarette while they walk up to a street, that is a taxi rank but the only thing that is malodorous, the smell coming from what I am about to show you. The doors to the row of taxis are open, the first one is the front passenger side door that's open, they walk past having nothing going on inside, they don't stop to check the back, if there is someone inside they would let them know. The second silver eight-seater they can see through the front window, with a bloodied smeared hand which brings your vision to the Indian taxi driver slumped over the steering wheel, with the side of his head eaten away, what is left of his brains spilling out, from his cracked skull he has acquired, they get to the back of the cab door half open, a lady is laying on her back with her guts ripped out, tits out.

George says " She was hoping to get lucky tonight."

Adam asks " How you know that?"

George responds saying " She has her flange out mate, no knickers or thong."

Tony without hesitation nearly slipping as he turns to look, Adam isn't closely behind to look.

George says " Lads she is dead, what you going to do take a pic."

Adam says " Nah, of course not."

As he puts his phone back into his jeans.

Tony says " Such a waste, looks nice to taste.

They re-join Shane that is alongside George approaching the third, that has the back door slid fully open to the black eight-seater cab, with the smartly dressed bald Z cab driver, he is on all fours eating his human dinner, as George is waving his hand down, after starting to crouch walk, the bald head of the Z starts to grow hair with every piece of flesh it swallows. George notices this out of the corner of his eye but doesn't want to stick around, to get to know why this is happening or how the Z become without hair on his head in the first place. They cross over the road going between two taxis, more of them in the line but not wanting to find out what is in the other taxis, looking in the front of the other taxi as they stop in the gap, seeing the white taxi driver, could be English or Polish or even Scottish who knows, has had his cheek bitten off, blood has seeped from a knife wound in his forehead. George stepping forward, noticing the taxi drivers door is wide open. A person on a black bike just swerves, missing the four of them, but most probably most importantly not crashing into, the cab drivers side door along with the female Z, a hammer still sticking out of her skull, Adam's phone light highlights blood had seeped out of the Z's head from the hammer blow, some bike tire trails visible in the settling snow, she is laying on her side with her black snowy trainers poking out from under the front bumper, should of spotted that. The cyclist doesn't stop, he has long gone. They walk down the same back way that Bobby took Tracy.

Bobby walking with Tracy towards the Grafton center, being quiet because of the bodies that lay on the ground, don't know if they are dead or undead. They do not have many weapons just the corkscrew along with Bobbies muscles, that are still to be put to the test, see just like Tony you can have all the muscles you like, but in these situations if you can't fight, your fucked. Bobby nearly treads with all his weight on to a black object submerged in to the snowy coating, like icing sugar dusted over a cake. Bobby picks up the dark object, brushes away the snow it's a smart phone. He clicks the circular button, the home screen lights up, with a couple kissing at a mountains mouth, he just gets a glimpse at the time before noticing the one percent battery in the corner. After the phone powers down. He puts this in his back trouser pocket, after tells Tracy.

"It is seven minutes past three."

They carry on walking towards the front of the Grafton center.

Tracy Says "I am hungry also thirsty."

Bobby response is "Same, let us look in the shopping center."

Lucky for the pair the doors are still open, they normally lock it at a certain time of night, to keep the homeless out from sleeping within. The doors are opening then to quickly shut on the already crushed head of a person, like a watermelon that has repeatedly been hit by a sledge hammer, while the body lay inside the shopping centre. Bobby does the Jesus cross over himself, while Tracy winces. They can hear from somebody eating, when I say eating I mean the disgusting type, like slurping spaghetti in the pasta sauce shite. They look to their right to see outside of a closed bank, is a smartly dressed person laying dead with half of his brains laying out over the pavement. Seeing a coating of snow all Around To twO Z's feast, starting now.

tHE FIRSt ONe CroUcheD oVer eatinG the MAns
intestines, bLood goes dripPing doWn his chin, with
the other Z with its bacK to the pair, Bobby
alongside Tracy breaths QuietlY eXhales Joining each
other's, the second Z hunched over feasting on the
brains of their victims, keeping it as an exclusive
meal.

You now can clap, finishing here.

After the first few brain portions go into the
second Zs mouth, the second Z straightens up as the
rotten flesh on its face starts to heal, his eyes
start to regain their rightful colour. He starts
sniffling as he envisioning the guys life, of the
brain he is eating.

What the Z is envisioning is the guy, seeing this
through his eyes, he is rushing through the airport
with his girlfriend, one hand pulling his luggage
while the other is reaching out for his lady's hand,
he turns his head to see her, dark hair swaying while
she is rushing beside, her hand trying to reach out
for his, her red lipstick sticking out on her lips,
one of her smiles can bring happiness to life, not
just his life but everyones life that she come into
touch with, as their hands clasp together, as they
are weaving around people.

It jumps to when they are on an airplane, she has
taken her seat, but he is standing putting his bag
in the overheads, wearing a grey t' shirt. While
speaking with her but the words are muffled, her eyes
as dark as a well on a dark night, you could easily
get lost in them, she scrapes her hair back to flick
behind her ear, while giggling at something he just

said. As he sits down beside her to hold her hand, her fingers locking with his, an engagement ring on her finger, they kiss.

It skips forward, to them at the place where that picture on the phone that Bobby found was taken, as the guy is giving someone his phone after the couple go to stand in front of the mountain. But the visual effects that the Z is experiencing abruptly stop because the other Z that was munching on the guys intestines is on the move barging past to go get what he has spotted, you would think this would be Bobby along Tracy but turning to see them not there anymore, well you would be gone.

Bobby along with Tracy are walking through the shopping center, I shouldn't have to tell you but there is all the big name brands shops throughout. Over there shoulders is still the entrance with the body laying on the ground, the doors still opening then shutting, but the body has stopped jolting because there is nothing left of the persons head, anyway back to it, Tracy points to a sign on the wall, which there is toilets upstairs, they don't want to make too much noise because they don't have much to defend themselves. Bobby puts his thumb up, so they decide to take the stairs.

At the same time as they go to the toilet, George with the others are walking past the back entrance of the bus station, to a poorly lit path, all their senses are on high alert because they can hardly see none of the surrounding area, the snow still heavily falling, just about making some of the outlines of

objects out in the surrounding area, they come to
the first ray of light flickering down from a
lamppost, but doesn't help all that much. They walk
out from the light like a flickering spotlight on a
stage. You would be fucked if you had epilepsy. Their
different paired trainers crunching in the settled
snow with each step they take. They approach the next
flickering light, but the noise from the weather
elements along with their shuffling feet is
interrupted by a scared lady scream They abruptly
stop walking to listen, squinting.

George whispers asking " Which way do you think
that scream come from?"

Adam responds in the same type of tone, " I think
it came from the way we are going."

They carry on walking to their first beam of light
that isn't flickering from this lamppost, not sure
if it is good or bad thing for them, as long as they
follow the lampposts they will get to the Grafton
center. Before they can leave the light. . .

Like a bowling ball speedily hitting its
designated pins for a strike, a Z jumps out of the
darkness around the light, to bowl down the group of
four. Minly taking Tony out but not in a nice way
for a spot of brunch dear, well the Zs kind of dinner.
Rolling across the ground his clothes becoming snowy
but body heat causing melting into his clothes so
they become soggy, but they can't lay on the ground
for too long making snow angels, there is a Z that
wants to chomp on their behinds. As the three of them
quickly make it to their feet to regroup, just Adam
still out in the darkness.

George saying out loud " Fucking Adam"

But he soon re-joins scaring the life out of them Adrenaline rushing now as they only have a split second before they can see the Z, it can come from anywhere, they are armed with their knives. . .

At the same time Bobby is washing his hands in the toilets sink, his palm presses the soap dispenser, rubbing his hands together. Rinsing them hearing in the ladies toilets the hand dryer being used. Bobby decides not to use them in the gents, not to wake up anymore Zs before he leaves the toilets, he is looking in the mirror, seeing in the reflection the urinals, a man either dead, drunk, Z or alive laying facedown in the urinals, the fourth option is unlikely though, for the obvious reason somehow Bobby had to have a piss, he is adjusting his bouncer card in his right sleeve, water seeping into his trousers fabric as dries his hands on them

He joins Tracy outside the toilets, not a soul in sight, well not until they get to the top of the stairs, looking down to the bottom, a female Z lay over the first step slowly climbing up.

Bobby says whispering " That wasn' t there before. "

Tracy whispers asking " How do we get around that?"

Ding " Level one, the toilets."

Is spoken by a female voice that comes from inside the elevator at the side.

Bobby whispers " That will do."

They go to walk over there, the big metal elevator doors open, a blood thirsty Z comes manically running towards the pair. Bobby with the corkscrew between his middle also marriage finger with with his grip tightening around its metal leaver, like brass knuckles. One time Bobby punches the Z in his face, the corkscrew drills between the flesh eaters eyes, like a barbed hook, when the Z drops to the ground, it yanks the corkscrew out from his hand. Tracy just standing shocked but before they can go to the elevator to avoid the corpse at the bottom of the stairs. In all the commotion the corpse grabs ahold of Bobby' s ankle. The Z is soon to let go of his ankle because his size ten steel toecap boot, nearly takes the female Zs head clean off her shoulders, but instead she is falling down the stairs with her chin bouncing off every step. They quickly rush into the lift before more Zs show up, looking at the panel on the lift wall, a bloody hand smeared down the panel, not knowing how the Z virus spreads. Bobby runs over to corkscrew Z, to see if he there is a piece of clothing he can use protect his finger, to press the button. His eyes scanning over the truly deceased ex Z, all pieces are bloodied so instead Bobby puts his index finger up at Tracy, to indicate one minute.

Tracy asks quietly " That long?"

Bobby smirks after he turns walking off to the toilets.

he responds " Not since my teenage years, over excited with too much foreplay."

Tracy smiles as he goes back in to the gents, the lift doors go to close in front of her eyes, her visibility of the toilet doors hallway are restricting until she reaches out, swiping her hand between the closing doors, they start to slowly re-open.

At the same time to George, that is with the others which have ran through the snowy semi lighted pathway, different types of trees like giants standing guard either side, but they are empty of leaves you will have to wait until early May to see what trees these are. to the last lamppost lighting beaming down on them, a figure comes running towards, into the light. Someone has to stop everyone from being the brain munchers next meal. George jabs the figure with his cricket bat, white willow wood thumps into his chest to keep the Z at bay, after George swings it back to take the figures head off mate, but the figure is clutching his chest, dropping to his knees while agony is clearly leaving their existence. The lads all look at each other.

Shane says " That' s the first time I have seen a Z being hurt."

George responds saying " Yeah same, maybe they do have feelings."

The short brown haired with blue highlights figure tilts their head up to reveal feminine facial features, piercing on both ears along with a nose ring piercing on her left nostril.

While clutching her right boob, she says with pain in her voice, " That was uncalled for."

George responds saying " Was it fuck! Could have been a Z, saying that there is one still about."

Shane asks " I bet you feel like a right tit mate?"

Before George can say another word, or introduce themselves to this young lady, a groan comes from behind Tony' s left shoulder, the Z emerges from the darkness. Tony as stiff as a mannequin until he carefully reaches out, to grab ahold of the green

handled knife that Adam is passing. While George is
pointing at what shoulder the Z is dribbling on, I
am sure he can hear the Z snarling, but you don't
know what other people's hearing is like. The Z like
a vampire, his rotting mouth opens ready to strike,
but before its blood craving teeth with pieces of
flesh stuck between, can sink in to Tony's neck.
Someone get him a toothpick, Tony turns as soon as
his hand grips the handle, quickly hooking the Z with
the blade slicing into his temple to his rotting
brain, lucky Tony is right handed, lights out for
the Z that is soon to feel for a split second the
snowy floor, his muscles have finally come into some
use, we will leave them for a few minutes while they
introduce themselves, to carry on with their journey
to the Grafton center. The new member of their team
is called Skyla, by the way.

Back to the toilets where Tracy is still in the
lift, the heavy metal doors opening back up, the
gents toilet door breaks opens the wrong way, the
cause for this is Bobby throwing a Z, that I presume
was taking a dump, because of his trousers also
boxers are around his ankles, through it followed by
himself, with some force. A man that throws people
out from night clubs for a living, just tossed this
Z like it was nothing. Full on carnage within a
matter of seconds. Bobby makes it back to his feet,
the Z doesn't have the same kind of luck because of
a shard of door that is sticking out from his head.
He is dusting himself while walking back to Tracy in
the lift, pulling some tissue out from his pocket.
    Bobby saying " Got what we needed. "

He is pressing the blood smeared panel, hopefully getting the ground floor button, looking at the Z, blood leaking down the shard of wood from his head wound.

A woman's voice breaks the silence " Lift going down."

Tracy says " That's a good start."

The doors are shutting while Bobby drops the bloody tissue.

Back to the now group of five, after everyone has introduced themselves, they walk through the traffic lights, that divides town centre where they come from, to the Grafton centre where they are going. They can hear smacking on some glass coming from somewhere, most probably from a Z trapped in a car, but visibility still a problem also they don't want to put themselves in more danger. Adam presses the traffic light button, as he walking faster to catch up, over the crossing, just about seeing the flashing green man through the heavy snow.

The lift doors open to reveal the basement of the shopping centre, but lucky for the pair it is lit up like a Christmas tree on Christmas Day. Bobby is the first to enter the basement followed by Tracy, to reveal a long hallway straight ahead, but eventually turns up ahead.

Tracy says " We need to get weapons."

Bobby responds saying " We need to first find the stairs back to the ground level, also food."

As he says that his stomach rumbles or it could be a Z around the corner of the hallway. They walk down the corridor to venture into the unknown.

Two lads are sitting at the bus depot, sheltering from the cold snowy weather, they seem oblivious to what is going on around them, as they are passing a joint between themselves. There is a two buses parked up, but there isn't any activity from inside, there could be a maximum of five buses parked up here at once, these buses are used to take people within the city to other cities.

George alongside the others have arrived, at the place Bobby got Tracy her new pumps. The snowing has started to ease off. There are bodies everywhere but the only problem is, they are not laying on the ground anymore, they are standing roaming around, while bumping into each other, some of the Zs meals are scattered around on the floor ahead of them, their guts spilled out with parts of brain, spilling out from their cracked skulls. A few of the Zs have their guts spilling out, while still roaming around because their heads are still intact, I guess it is true what they say, you must kill them by destroying their brains.

The Tomboy girl asks " Is there a less suicidal way around?"

George responds saying " Like the back of my hand, I know my city, follow me."

They walk left following George, their footsteps crunching in the settled snow, as they try not to disturb the roaming Zs because, the small hoard would destroy this small group.

Bobby with Tracy behind are walking up some steps towards a heavyset door, a small rectangular mesh window within the middle of the door, that Bobby stops at to look through.

Tracy asks " Anything?"

Bobby responds saying " Nothing at the moment sweetheart."

He cracks the door open a little to poke his head out, he looks both one way but sees nothing, he turns his his head to look up at a Zs rotting face, groaning at him Making Bobby jump he sharply opens the door outwards. It smashing into the Zs face, that flies backwards, on his bum sliding on the slippery laminated flooring until the wall stops the Z from sliding anymore. Bobby quickly rushes over to the Z that is trying to make it back to its feet, but Bobby's boot crashing through his head, like kicking a carved out pumpkin. There is pieces of flesh, skull mixed with brains scattered everywhere, exploding up the wall. Tracy emerges out from the basement door while Bobby is checking if the area is clear. Lucky for them there is no more Zs around even luckier for them they have come out near a open, but empty from people, Costabucks coffee shop. They start start taking sandwiches along with drinks from the refrigerated unit, that is half been shut with half that looks like it's been broken in the rush of the Z virus spreading. Bobby clearly not picky about what sandwich he picks up, he tears open the sandwich packaging, wolfing down the sandwich after drinking half a sugary drink. Tracy a bit more lady like in the way she eats, even taking a seat at one of the many empty tables, one that hasn't got half filled coffee cups along with crisp packets or chocolate bar wrapper, my personal favorite are the Kinder B or Kitty Kat Chunky, both of them with a cup of tea, lovely like a slice of heaven.

The small group are sneaking down a side alley between two walls that belong to big brand shops, they come out from the alley, at the entrance of the Grafton shopping center, they have to not be spotted by a Z because they are now deep in their new territory. A snarl in exchange for words every time the Zs bump into each other. George followed by the others are stealth walking to the shopping center entrance, they steadily walk past the body with the squashed head, into the shopping center via the other entrance, that is beside. They are not long through the entrance undetected, but unfortunately they can be as sneaky as they want, but they cannot hide their human scent. Which a snarling Z has just picked up from them, he sniffs the air after sees them venturing through the other side of the automatic glass doors. The Z runs limping towards them, but doesn't wait for the automatic doors to open, so the Z just plows through the glass door, that should be bullet proof but I don't think it is, as the shards of glass shatter outwards, slowly followed by the Z, slow motion as both explode after drop to the floor, this alerts the small group which are at the toilet stair entrance, they start to jog away to find a place to hide, but what is unbeknown to them, it has also alerted the small hoard outside to start to chase after them

As they are running through the shopping center, dodging bins, some shops haven't got their shutters down, with lights still on. The rest running ahead of George, that side steps a grey shopping center bin, after skidding around the corner, nearly clambering into a shops display window, I swear he was that close even the sexy dressed mannequins nearly flinched. He is quick to quietly call the others back because he has spotted something. As the others stop, jogging to look back to see George waving them back, because through the shops display is a slit, that he is peering through to see, a lady with her tits out, fingering herself, only joking my friend it's two Zs banging on a white office door.

George whispers " Come on, they will be closed. "

Adam tries to whisper back but not sure why he tried, his voice is deep like the core of this very earth, with every decibel saying " I think it's too late, it is like a ghost town. "

George responds " Yeah alright, voice! Tone it down, look. "

He points to the two Zs, still trying to get into the office door, fuck knows how they didn't hear Adams voice. A clothes shop is Next to a cookie shop. Three casual dressed mannequins each side of the open shops entrance. Now I am telling you this because you will see my friend, the group of five are interrupted by the small hoard of Zs that are rushing through the shopping center, as they spill around the corner, turning back to see the five humans have disappeared. The small hoard come rushing through turning round the corner towards the cookie shop, after turning again after going to explore the rest of the shopping center. The two Zs that was banging on the office door are now joining the hoard, which isn't good for anyone that comes into contact with the brain suckling dickheads. George's breath is released from his lips, as his eyes check to see if the coast is clear. Let me draw your eyes out so you can see the bigger picture, the five of them was posing as mannequins in the clothes shop Next to the cookie shop. They all have funny poses, with the actual mannequins laying at their feet.

Back to the bus depot, where the two lads are sitting, an exhale of smoke mixed with the cold nights air from the first lads mouth, as he drops the finished smoke to the floor, his buddy notices one of the bus doors is open.
The first lad is Jerry, his mate is called Tomas.
Jerry says " I wonder if the keys are still in the ignition."
Tomas response is " There is only one way to find out."
They both stand up to go check out the bus.

Back to the group putting the casually dressed mannequins back upright. Adam laughs out loud as he puts his one in a striking pose, George puts his ones index finger up its nostril, on the other hand is the middle finger fully erected, pointing outwards. After they climb out from the display area.
George says " Let us go check out what the Zs was banging the door for."
They all walk further into the shop, passing cloths racks, towards the office door at the back...

Why don' t we go see what the other two are doing, Bobby taking a swig of water, from a mineral spring somewhere in a secret mountain, of course it isn' t tap water they wouldn' t lie, pull the wool over anyones eyes. Anyway back to it my friend this story won' t tell itself, Bobby puts the cap back on the water bottle.

Tracy while putting her half eaten chicken salad sandwich, on the packaging.

She asks " Do you think this has over spilled?"

Bobby responds saying " I hope not, I have a family. I just want us to survive this night, with daylight it will be better to assess the damage. "

Tracy just about to respond but they can hear some noise getting closer with every millisecond that is passing. The small hoard comes speeding around the corner, some splattering into the shops windows, like insects hitting a speeding car, looking back to the table the pair are sitting at, is now empty with the wooden coffee shop chair rocking. Their rubbish still on top of the table, as the hoard is passing through, if it' s in their way it' s getting wrecked.

In the meantime at the sniper tower. Mr Officer is looking down the scope, inspecting the wall, stopping any Zs that are trying to get to any fair workers, that are inside. A pair of armed police officer are going to the closed entrance, covering each other' s backs. The entrance is quickly opened to let the pair in, a couple of seconds pass with the illuminating lights being switch off. A voice comes over the snipers radio saying " Keep a look out, especially around the wall. "

As the last bit of the voice over the radio is speaking, there is gunshots, that the sniper sees through his scope, bullets tearing through the skull of an approaching Z. He looks around the wall but only seeing dead Zs laying around, blood seeping from their wounds. The sniper stops looking for a second, having a swig from his drink that was on the ledge. While he takes in the beauty of the town centre, he spots something turning around the corner. He looks through his scope to get a closer look, it's a fucking bus being driven by someone.

The sniper radios over to the police officer below asking " Why are the buses still running?"

A voice comes back out from the police radio saying " It is four in the morning, they shouldn't be."

The sniper looks again through his scope following the bus, trying to get a closer look at who is driving.

Going on the bus with Tom, as high as a kite taking the bus for a drive around, with Jerry coming down the stairs after checking the rest of the double decker out for people, but clearly not finding nothing. The window wipers are clearing the snow.

Jerry says " Everything looks clear bro."

As he picks up a free newspaper that the bus company provides, flicking through the pages.

Tom calls back " Happy days brother, I wonder why the keys was left in the ignition, without the keys being taken with him or her, I am not sexist."

Jerry responds asking " Fuck knows, but I am glad it was because how many times do you get to take a bus for a spin around town?"

Jerry puts the newspaper back after joins Tom at the front, holding onto the metal bars, for folks to move around the bus, like a monkey swinging from branches, as the wheels goes over a sleeping policeman. If you don't know what a sleeping policeman is then search it, educate yourself please.

As Tom accelerates going down this tight road, every so often bumping over a sleeping policeman.

Tom responds saying " That is true, apart from if you' re a bus driver then nearly everyday. "

Jerry nods as he is looking through the big window. As the bus turns right round a hotel corner.

The two police officers are inside of the winter fair, sitting down at a table while the lady of the fair, a hefty woman hands them a cup of tea. The man of the fair with grubby fingerless gloves on, blowing the steam from his hot cup of char, after taking a slurp.

The man asks saying " The dead has come back to life you say?"

The Mexican police officer takes his hat off, after puts sugar in his hot cup of drink.

After the officer responds saying " That is exactly what my partner has just told you, you will have to secure this place. "

The English police officer asks " Where' s your toilets?"

The lady says " We have a portable one, that' s behind our caravan. "

The English police officer asks " Thanks, you don' t mind?"

The man of the fair responds saying " Help yourself, Officer. "

After he gets up to go there.

The bus turns the corner, running into a male Z, he was smartly dressed, I would presume he was on a night out with friends. Slowing this down to see the full force of the front of the bus crashing into the

Z, with the lads expressions that are inside of the bus. Tom slams on the brakes but it is too late the damage is done as the dead Z rolls away while the bus comes to a emergency stop. Tom presses a button that opens the bus doors, Jerry is quick to get out, so he can make sure the person is alright. Unbeknown to him or both of them that a Z virus has spread. A gunshot sounds on the tranquil night soon after, Jerry is quick to run back into the bus.

While panicking shouting " Drive bro! Fucking drive!"

His urgency sparks Tom into action, as he puts the bus in gear after quickly drives off.

Tom asks " What happened?"

Jerry trying to calm his nerves by shakily rolling a roll up, as he is explaining what happened....

So let me show you what happened as soon as Jerry steps off the bus. He starts looking around to see where the body is, but at first can' t see nothing, only tire marks in snow until he hears scraping, the Z comes crawling round the corner. Half of its face rotten off, legs looking like they have been Roy Keane tackled. Jerry is too focused on the Z crawling on the floor to notice another Z that is slowly prowling towards the stunned Jerry. Slowing it down to see, a bullet bursts out from the strolling Zs forehead, which snapped Jerry back to the land of living, because it wisps past his ear. Well the rest you know because he didn' t stick around, to find where bullet come from

The English police officer is unlocking the portable toilets door after finishing his piss, he starts walking towards the four bed caravan, creamy complexion. Cream net curtains that stop full visibility into their home. The police officer is adjusting himself dusting off his heavy black bullet proof vest. He walks up to the caravan windows, Being nosy he peeks in, to see a lad in his mid-twenties sprinkling a powder substances over candy floss, after repackaging them to sell for children to consume or even adults. This is what grabs his eye but what really grabs his attention is faint knocking coming from inside a red shipping container, you know the big ones they have at the docks, well there is one not far away from the portable toilet. The police officer goes over to it, placing his ear beside he hears...

A faint female voice from inside asking " Can you let me out please M? I need toilet."

The English police officer quickly looks around to see if he has been spotted, but he hasn' t so he decides to....

The police officer arrived back to his partner, that is speaking with the fair owners, a married couple.

The Mexican police officer asks " Is it just you two?"

The deserted shut down rides lay dormant around the fair ground, during the day they bring joy to all the kids.

The man puts his cup down on the table, as he responds saying " No our son is in our caravan."

The English police officer is typing something on his mobile.

The Mexican police officer asks " Is it just you three that run this place everyday?"

The woman is just about to respond but her husband beats her to it by saying, " No we have another family that help out, but they have needed to go out of town, family emergency."

By the looks of it he wanted to cover up a secret, my bet is that they use locals to avoid certain laws.

He puts his phone on his partners lap, the Mexican police officer glances down to read the message written in text form, after looks up at the couple while the English police officer takes his mobile back.

The Mexican police officer asks " You don' t mind if we take a look around, you know just so we feel safe."

The mans response is to say " Of course you can look around Cuntstable." (I know it' s not the correct spelling.)

The owner agree so they don' t look suspicious.

Bobby is with Tracy still, both are hiding behind the coffee shop counter, having just heard a noise. Not knowing if it is the hoard coming back but they are soon to realize it isn' t because of whispers, that is coming from the small group that George is apart of. Slowly Bobby hunched over the counter, to see George is speaking with a pretty blond haired lady, that is dressed in retail attire, she was the one that was hiding in the office. The others are following behind, making sure they are observant so no Z or Zs get the jump on them, Tracy sitting on the floor beside Bobby' s leg.

" We should check Costalot over there to see if there is a drink or food or both, I am not fussy. " Adam whispers.

They head over there to Costalot as Bobby kneels back down behind the counter, whispering to Tracy " Stay still, don' t know the intentions of these people. "

Tracy nods as the group come over to fridge to take what they need. George lights a cigarette while taking a seat as others join him Bobby looking around the ground to find anything he can use as a weapon, his eyes dart on to an clean but chipped Costalot mug, you know the big ones, maybe your drinking out of it now, well when they open back up, that has the coffee café logo printed on its side, he grabs ahold of gripping it tightly, poised at any second to strike.

George is looking around while smoking his cigarette, retail shops all around.

Tony asks " Do you think there is any other survivors?"

Adam says " I hope so, imagine if this is it for the rest of our lives, we have to rebuild civilization. "

Tony responds on genuine disgust. " Nah It can' t be, no more going out on a night out, taking some bird for a quickie then waking up next to her friend in the morning, having to do the walk of shame. "

Adam says " More like the walk of legends. "

They both laughing like naughty boys up to mischief, as they fist bump. Even the hiding Bobby has a smirk on his face.

George using his finger to map out a plan on the table, also pointing out places.

While saying " Let's go to explore the rest of Grafton after go back, from the top half, we can go through the automatic doors over here, if they are open. After go down a back alley that will lead us near Primarni, if you know where that is then good, only problem is we will be exposed, so cover each other backs."

Hannah, the retail girl asks " Is there toilets up there."

While doing the pee dance.

George responds asking " Yes, they are up the escalator, any more questions?"

Shane asks " The hoard is...?"

George stood up, leaning back to see around the corner wall of a woman's clothes shop, cuts in to say " Coming, everyone hide."

Everyone scatters, hiding as the hoard is trotting back on the hunt for human flesh. Adam dives behind the counter where he is soon greeted by Bobby that is still hiding with Tracy. Adam laying on the ground, his eyes flickering between both of them Bobby drags him towards them both, he has got to have some power to do that in his arm because Adam is not exactly a small geezer, after putting his finger to his lips " Shhhh."

The hoard is quick to pass but not without sniffing around like a shit police dog hunting for drugs, didn't find nothing.

Everyone emerges from their hiding places, George with the two ladies walk back to the table, Shane along with Tony are the next to walk over to the table. George takes another cigarette out from his pocket, after looking around.

He is asking " Where is Adam?"

Tracy in the middle of Bobby on her left, Adam on her right emerge from behind the counter.

Bobby asks " Bro, please give me a smoke, ran out on my shift, I could smell your one earlier, nearly popped my head out."

George chucks him the pack after lights his cigarette.

He asks " You have been there the whole time?"

Bobby taking a smoke from the packet after responds saying " Yeah since before the hoard first passed through."

George passes him the lighter while responding asking " Okay then you heard the plan?"

Bobby nods after lights his cigarette, takes a drag after exhales.

George says " Good, up to if you want to come, also keep the packet."

Bobby puts the packet in his pocket after responds asking " Much Appreciated, you have somewhere to hold up?"

George responds saying " Yeah, a restaurant on bridge street."

Tracy excitingly says " Let's go then, what are we waiting for."

Tony looking smitten over Tracy as he responds saying " Took the words out of my mouth."

They all take what they can for from the fridge, stuffing their pockets, after go the way George said, back to the restaurant.

All of them make it back to the restaurant
unscathed, all of them wait it out there, drinking,
eating, smoking until the sun rises, early around
seven in the morning.

At the police roadblocks around the towns
outskirts, they have survived all night, containing
the Z virus within, people that travel in to cities
town centre to work are being told to go home, wait
inside their homes until further notice. Big delivery
trucks are being sent away, not a single soul is
being allowed in unless they already are in there.
The roads need to be clear for the army to pass
through.
Which they do clearing out every nook to cranny
making sure all the Zs are killed, all survivors
rescued, all dead disposed of correctly.

The End...

Only joking I can't end it there, so many
questions you will have.

Where do I start, before the army turnt up, turning
the show to a blood bath, with bullets ripping
through the dead's heads, X-ray mode. Anyway let me
take you to the two coppers that was intruding in
the fair owners business. There, look! one of
officers currently having his brains eaten by a
female Z, by the looks of the ripped open bloody face
it is the Mexican police officer. The Z stops as the
mushed brain is going down its gullet. It sniffs the
cold early morning air while being introduced for a
short while to the Mexican police officers life.

The vision the Z is experiencing is, the English police officer is calling out to his partner " Raul, we have a call, let' s go. "

Raul gets up from his office chair, he kisses his two fingers after places them on to a photo of his family, that is framed, beside his computer.

It is the same night as the Z virus spread, he is with his partner, arms fully extended, gun in hands letting bullets fly to hit the oncoming Zs. The Z that is experiencing Raul' s life vision is also feeling the adrenaline what Raul was feeling. Adrenaline is soon to change to compassion, as he is looking down to see a friend of his missus. He remembers that she works in the city, but unfortunately she didn' t make it out because her skin is peeling from herself, claret engulfed the whites of her eyes, a ferocious expression explodes from her face, so Raul puts her out from the misery, that has inundated her life. As a bullet explodes out from the back of her head.

Skipping forward to when he is sitting beside his partner, glancing down to see the message on his partners phone, which reads ' I see in their caravan, their lad sprinkling white powder over candy floss also there is people inside a container. '

As the rest of the scene plays out which is what you witnessed earlier.

It fast forwards a little to them having their gun in one hand, crossed over is a torch, shining in their other hand. As the light scans over different rides until they get to a caravan, what you didn't notice is the man of the fair, done some knocks on the caravans side, they have a few different style of knocks meaning different things. The caravan door opens to reveal the lad with a shotgun pointing towards the policeman.

The lads name is Ryan, slicked back black hair says " Give my old mans your guns, take your belts along with bullet proof vest off."

The police officers comply with what they are told to do, as the man that owns the fair, snatches their guns only to point their guns at them

Now letting the coppers go through the front, would be stupid because they would come back with more old bill, or killing them well that is past stupidity. So let the Zs kill them right, correct. There is a back door that Ryan leads them to, with the shotgun barrel poking in their back, switching between both of them the old man beside his son. Raul looking at the few approaching Zs, with skin pealing with their jaws ferociously snapping at the moment thin air, but a few seconds could be flesh. Raul silently speaking a prayer, but his lights are soon put out like his partners, not because the holy words saved him because the gun butts connection with the back of their heads. The coppers drop to the ground, unconscious like giving change to the homeless. The rest is known to you because the Zs are in the process of eating them but what isn't known to you is, if the police men was left to stay alive, they would of stumbled across an underground city for the Asian nationals that get into England, for a better life at a price but they don't need a visa to live in the underground city. The fair owners are only a small cog within this operating operation, but if any authority stumble upon this, it is dangerous, well the sprinkle of white powder over candy floss, is to keep people coming back, somehow.

I am sure you are wondering what happened to Tom also Jerry, they are still alive as the army stormed into the bus, while they are sharing a joint among themselves.

Of course the star of the show George well, the army was going through Bridge Street as the sun is rising. After being cleared free from the Z virus, he stole a bike from a bike alley to arrive at his daughters home in time to take her to out for the day, but not before having some kind of a wash, he still had to run most of the way to make it on time.

Now the visual story is finished, oh yeah before I go. The last question I have to answer, the cause of the Z virus was contaminated meat from the lamb burger, it could' ve happened anywhere in any city, but it happened at Bridge Street, David2Marseille. What a night!

Through His Eyes

Welcome, take a seat! Get comfortable my friend watch this story come to life in comfort until the end.

Sausages sizzling in their frying pan on top of a gas run white stove, a fork stabs into the meat, the porks juices run out like my football team onto their home pitch, as they are turned, to get the other side more crispy. Looking back to reveal the bigger picture, a lady, her back to us with tied up curly rich chestnut hair, in her white dressing gown, is dancing to songs which are playing out from their grey radio in the corner of their worktop. She is cooking a fry up for her fella that has been working all night at the local fire station. In this sleepy town of Sovereign, their last fire was in the towns only forest many, many moons ago, caused by a campfire also teenage kids smoking along with drinking, but during the day they aid surrounding towns or cities. But at night they only have one fireman or firewoman on, just in case something goes down or is burning down but unlucky for this woman it was her fella, that was on last night.

She is Samantha, her hair swaying from her dance moves. Performance is underway, in a happy mood. As she places the cooked sausages on a white plate, her sweat voice singing the lyrics of the song playing. She goes to the grey sexy fridge, you know the one I mean, with the ice dispenser, expensive but worth it, but that's not the point. She opens the fridge getting the pack of bacon out, shutting their half full fridge, filled with different products which are stored correctly, she stabs the packet with a serrated knife, opening. The water inside their black kettle is boiling, steam floating out from where the water is poured from, along with specs of boiling water spitting out because the kettle has been over filled, Samantha never follows the correct level. Placing the first rasher in their frying pan, bacon sizzling in the same oil that come from the cooked sausages, as Samantha lays the second rasher of bacon down. She quickly washes her hands after drying them with kitchen towel, she pours the boiled water into their teas.

A knock on the door reaching Samantha's ear, she turns the stoves knob around, turning it off so she doesn't burn her place down. Reaching over turning the radio down after she goes to hallway, looking down making sure she hasn't got a boob out, she ties her dressing gown properly around her waist. She opens her white front door...

A police officer stands at her doorstep with a glum expression on his face, as he takes his hat off.
Samantha says asking "Hi Justin, you alright?"

Justin is a friend of theirs, a tear streams down his cheek his bushy brown mustache of his full beard, soaks up his streaming tear.

He chokes up a little as he says "Err, oh shit Samantha, Sam's, ugh."

He nearly chucks up the contents within his stomach, after he wipes the few tears that are rolling down his cheeks, away.

Samantha asks "Sam's what?"

Even she is getting emotional but she doesn't know why.

You can hear the sadness in his voice, as he says, "There is no easy way to say this, Sam was pronounced dead this morning."

Samantha's jaw drops open in disbelief, head drops as she starts crying in her hands, couldn't even hold it back. Justin grabs ahold of her shoulders after brings her in to him, giving Samantha a tight hug.

Samantha has invited Justin in, she is sitting in her chair as he sits in the middle, on the edge of her sofa.

Samantha sobbing her precious heart out, asks "How? How did this happen? What happened?"

Tears streaming down Justins face, he takes a tissue out from the box on their coffee table, after passes her the box.

So let's go to the early hours of this morning, Sam a stocky geezer, with styled black hair, clean shaven. He is walking up the stairs of the fire station, black boots stepping on each step, climbing further up. Until he gets to the door at the top, walking through into their mess room, not much is inside just a tattered old sofa, which Sam normally falls asleep on, after he does his checks around the station, also the fire truck, that is underneath this room. Sam goes over to the sofa sitting down, taking his boots off. While he takes them off let me explain the rest of the room. Against the wall is a desk, no chair just a few bits of papers scattered around along with a old styled dirty white telephone in the corner. Opposite that is a window, the best thing in this room there is a football table top against the wall opposite the sofa, but it is a battered one, the lads play when there is nothing, only time to kill. Sam places his boots at the side after lays down the sofa, puffing his grey t'shirt to let the air pass through because this room can get warm. Crossing his arms closing his eyes to sleep.

Samantha now dressed properly , she is in the back of the paddy wagon, that Justin is driving. A ladies voice comes over the police radio but Samantha drowns her voice out, while she is still sobbing, looking out of the police car window. As people are going about their day oblivious on the pain that Samantha is feeling. The car takes a right corner half way down the road, driving past the half burnt down fire station, the scorched wooden flooring failing to stay erect, like a fellas masturbating getting disturbed by a family member calling their name. The firefighters back away to not get trapped underneath this falling rubble. The police have cordoned the area off. As the scorched flooring crashes to the rubble below, the blackened melted football table top distinctively sticking out.

Ding "Basement floor." The female voice says from the elevator stopping.

Samantha standing beside Justin while the lift doors open. Clearing her tears away from her cheeks with a white tissue while Samantha follows Justin down a poorly lit corridor, to double doors at the bottom, that they walk through with Justin holding the door open for Samantha...

They are standing in the morgue, an older gent dressed in blue scrubs, a mouth mask doing its job covering his mouth. His old tired eyes peering through his glass lenses, at the naked body of a young lady, only pieces of cloth covering her genitalia. The older fella is cleaning the blood from the lifeless lady's face.

The older gent says "One minute please."

As he dips the blood soaked cloth in a metal silver bowl that's holding blood tinted water inside.

Justin says "This is Mr Preserve, he is our towns Diener, in his hay day a wonderful surgeon."

Samantha responds saying "Yeah I heard Sam mention him a few times."

Mr Preserve immediately stops what he is doing, putting the cloth beside the water bowl, that is on the same slab that the lifeless lady is laying on. After stands up while walking over to Samantha he takes his gloves off, dropping them in a bin, after grabs ahold of Samantha giving her a tight hug, like a dick penetrating a virgins pussy, rubbing her back as Samantha has waterfalls trickling out from her tear ducts.

Mr Preserve "Listen, I am truly sorry for your loss, he was a great man."

He rubs her hand while leading her over to the body fridges at the side of the room.

Mr Preserve "If you need time alone with him, we can go."

Samantha is cleaning her cheeks from tears with a now damp tissue, she shakes her head in a no gesture.

Mr Preserve says asking "Brace yourself, you sure you want to?"

Samantha nods while Justin is holding Samantha. Mr Preserve pulls the silver metal handle towards him, mist is escaping as the fridge door swings open. He pulls the body out that is covered by a white sheet. He lets go of the pole that he just pulled the body out by, Frost has melted away leaving his palm print, after he pulls the white sheet back. To reveal Sam, his burnt face, no hair because it was burnt in the fire, closed eyes although his appearance is horrible, he looks peaceful.

Samantha sobbing at the confirmation while repeating "Oh god, no, no, no baby, you can't be gone."

She kisses around the burns on his face after hugging his cold lifeless body, both men have a tears in their eyes.

Fast forward seven years to a university that is within the next town, of Aton. A group of five students three guys, two ladies, they are late teens. All share a mutual hobby, they are searching for their next adventure, sitting in the ladies uni room. One of the girls sitting on their bunk bed has a laptop on her lap. While at the desk ahead there are the lads, one sitting his laptop sits on top of her desk, the other two are standing either side of him.

Donald that is scratching his black bum fluffed chin while seated calls back to ladies "I think we have found something."

Angela hooks her brown hair behind her right pierced ear while asking "Where is it?"

Will the guy to Donald's left responds "In Sovereign, it happened a few years back."

Cameron itches his left blue eye lid while adding "Search for the fire in fire station of Sovereign."

Teresa the other lady responds saying "She is searching it now."

They are all having a few drinks because it's their last day of uni for the term, Will sparks his cigarette after takes ahold of his drink.

Angela says "We will go there tomorrow, it looks like it could be a scary one."

As the ladies read more, trying to get the whole back story.

The next day has risen as the five students are in Will's silver saloon car, he is driving, his parents brought him it. The students are on their summer holidays, they are on their way to the place where Sam was burnt to death. For the weekend they will explore the place for spirits, they all share the common interest in finding ghosts, or anything to do with the paranormal.

Teresa asks "The grounds keeper is gong to meet us there?"

Cameron beside her responds saying "Yes, he told us to meet him at the house by ten."

Angela that is trying to do her makeup in the car mirror as she asks "Why this early? I was trying to catch up on my beauty sleep."

Will squeezing tighter on his steering wheel getting white knuckle syndrome, while mumbling "Looks like your beauty sleeps is scared of you."

Angela asks "What was that babe?"

Will responds asking "Nothing, can you leave my rear view mirror alone please? You have one of them small girly ones, that you're normally pouting in."

While he is re-adjusting his mirror, Donald pulls a camcorder out from his backpack, as he is turning it on in the background.

They arrive at the site where seven years ago, see Sam burn to death. Now it is a massive five bedroom house, which the last family was quick to depart from. As Will parks up, tires pushing the gravel away as he reverses beside a black saloon car, with no one inside, but must be the groundskeepers motor. Everyone gets out of the car as Donald tries to get an up-skirt of Teresa with the camcorder, but only gets ass cheeks along with her pink thong.

Donald says "Cheeky one, you are."

Teresa disgusted, snappily responds saying "Fuck you."

He chuckles while getting out the other side, Cameron pops the boot, to get their stuff out. While they are doing this Will is checking out the black car.

He is looking in the back window while saying "Fuck, I should of got this car."

Teresa says "You mean your daddy should of brought you this one."

Will puts his middle finger up to her, as he walks around looking at the car head on, nodding while continue to say "Yeah, she looks sexily moody, if you ask me, have to appreciate that."

He notices something on the front passenger side seat. So he goes to investigate.

While Cameron in the background, shouting out "You could help!"

Will grumbles back "One moment."

While looking at the messy pieces of papers with all kinds news paper cut out articles, scattered all around the seat, but the thing that catches Will's eye, is a sentence scribbled in a corner of a news paper cutout, which reads "If you read this turn back now, leave!"

His concentration is broken by his mobile vibrate ringing, Will pulls his mobile out from his left pocket, a number that he doesn't recognize is showing so he taps the green phone on his mobile screen, that is next to the red phone to hang up. Putting the phone to his ear saying "Hello, this is Will speaking."

A voice on the other end responds saying "This is the groundskeeper, I am inside the house. Let yourselves in."

After the line goes dead, Will looks at the front of the house, seeing the top right bedroom cream curtain drop like someone was just watching them from there. Cameron from behind Will grabs ahold of both of his shoulders making him Jump.

As he asks "Who was that bro?"

Will at nearly having a heart attack.

Responds saying "Groundskeeper bro, he is inside said to let ourselves in."

So they both go to the boot of Will's car to help unload it, taking it into the house. His black trainers are pushing the gravel away with every step, with a bag in hand Will pushes the dark green front door open. As the others follow him in to house.

A breathtaking beautiful double staircases that leads up to the main center piece of a fucking spectacular gorgeous chandelier, I mean being brought up in a council flat we was lucky to have a lightbulb, or a lamp with a lightbulb beside my bed, if you know man, you know. Anyway enough of how I was raised with a candle flickering in the corner mate.

The lads put their bags down while in amazement, Will calls out for the groundskeeper, the ladies put their bags in the living room. Wills call out gets no response.

Will while admiring the front of the house display says "Wouldn't mind living in a place like this, imagine having one of these bad boys for yourself also family of course, another one for my mother."

Donald going off to the left, filming the spectacular dining room.

Cameron responds saying "Would be nice, of course one for me as well."

Will while chuckling says "Yeah no problem, if your paying, I would want them though without the possibility of them being haunted."

Cameron responds asking "Yes, but are you really alone?"

Will responds saying "I hope always especially when I am having a shit, not for my sake but for the spirits, poor fucker died just to die again.

They share a laugh while Teresa pokes her head around the door saying "Come see this."

Will asks "Is it the groundskeeper? because I need to find him before we make ourselves at home."

She responds saying "No just wanted to show you guys how beautiful this place is."

Will responds saying "I will come in a second, I'm going to find your man."

She hooks a thick strand of her hair over her ear as she responds saying "Hurry back."

Will walks towards the stairs as Cameron walks into the living room with Teresa.

Will is calling up "Hello, groundskeeper!"

But not a single soul responds as he reaches the top of the stairs, pictures still hanging up on the walls, hallways like the giants that used to rule this world lived here, fucking huge.

Some of the pictures of the smartly dressed family are portraits that have been painted, the others are camera took. He rings the number that was left on his phone, he puts it on the loud speaker, while it rings, a phone is ringing coming from one of the four doors, two each side of the massive hallway. Will walking to each room briefly putting his ear to each dark wooden door. None of them doors seem like they have the ringing coming from within, the ring tone eventually stops as it goes trough to the other phones voicemail. Verifying it must be the door right at the end of the hallway. Which he walks up to, opening it to reveal...

A stunning bedroom, imagine how you would want yours, then run with it that is how it looks. A phone at the end of the bed, on the fluffy carpet. The oil painted family portrait at the beds head above the headboard. Will walks in to retrieve the phone, he clicks on a button, the screen lights up to reveal the missed call from Will, along with the Mexican groundskeeper standing next to a beautiful flower bed, that he possibly planted looking happy with himself, as his phones wallpaper. Hearing a crackling noise, as he looks up the families portrait of the previous family that owned this house, has changed to the Mexicans groundskeepers family, from the bottom, it has started to catch fire, spreading to the hand carved ancient style gold frame, but it doesn't spread anymore than that, just staying within the frame as it crackles upwards, engulfing more of the painting, ashes twirling out from the painting.

Will says "Yeah, fuck that mate, I am gone."

Will turns to run out of the room to run out of the house, to leave the country most probably, but is stopped by Donald that he crashes into, he drops his camcorder with a thuds Into the carpet, now filming in the bedroom.

Donald asks "What's wrong?"

Will breathing heavily says "You can't see it?"

As he turns around to see the family portrait normal.

Will says "Well what's this bullshit then, it changed to the Mexican groundskeeper family, it started to burn, like actual fire burning the shit up bro, feels like my heart is going to explode out of my chest."

At the same time as Will is catching his breath along with calming his shit down, on the screen of the camcorder currently capturing the gruesome image of the groundskeeper, slumped at the bottom of the bed with a fireman's axe sticking out from his head. Donald picks up the camcorder.

Will asks "You still recording?"

Donald responds saying "Yes I have been recording since I got it out."

Will says "I am sure that will have it on there."

They both rush down stairs to tell the others what has just happened.

Will shouting "Guys, we found something!"

While he is walking down the stairs in front of Donald that is rewinding his camcorder.

The other three come from the living room while the camcorder rolls down the last three steps, hitting Wills foot that alerts him to it.

Will says "Be careful, we will need this as evidence."

He picks it up to look on the screen that is paused on the groundskeeper.

Will says "What the fuck! He wasn't there."

As the other three are asking "What?"

Cameron takes ahold of the Camcorder, as all three look at it.

Donald says "I see the picture burning as well."

Angela asks "What should we do?"

Cameron responds saying "We should go up there to help him."

Will responds asking "Help him? He had a fucking axe sticking out from his head, I have a funny feeling, he is passed help. I say we should save ourselves."

Teresa says "I would want someone to come back for me, to see if I am still alive."

Will says "If you have a axe sticking out from your head, I will not come back to check, I will presume you are dead, you know why because you have a fucking axe sticking out from your noggin mate, also his whole death appeared from thin fucking air."

Teresa says "Alright, calm down babes."

Donald takes the camcorder from Cameron while saying "We will go check."

They all start walking back up the stairs, Will clearly pissed off at the decision that has been made, huffing along with puffing all the way up the stairs.

All five arrive at the bedroom, the picture isn't burning or burnt, there also isn't no dead body.

Cameron asks "Where is he?"

The room shape shifts to the groundskeeper, lifeless with the axe slumped at the bottom of the bed, clutching his mobile in his hand. After a few seconds it goes back to normal.

Will checking his pockets for the groundskeepers mobile but can't find it, while panicky asks "You see that?"

Teresa says "Yes, that isn't like anything I have ever seen."

Cameron says "Me neither."

The room shape shifts again, this time, Sam with his back to them is pulling his axe from the groundskeeper skull, he is dressed in his fireman gear, which is burnt half into his skin, covering his left side to melted predominantly into the right side of him. After shape shifts back to normal for a few seconds, not long enough for the students to react with speech, before it shape shifts back to Sam, he has the groundskeeper over his right shoulder, with blood dripping from the gash in the groundskeepers head, droplets of blood dripping from the axes tip also his head gash. If you look closely in each blood drop you can see Samantha crying.

Sam smiles at the five students before he disappears with the groundskeeper along with his blood dripping axe, blood splatter up the bed also blood droplets soaking into the carpet.

Will says "Fuck that, I am out you can stay here."

He walks well more like scurries out of the room, missing steps as he goes down them towards the front door, picking his bags up on the way. The others are not far behind, he opens the front door to...

A mental asylums corridor with six doors either side, double doors at the bottom, from this far away looks to be locked with chains.

Will say angrily "When you think it can't get fucking worse, maybe if we shut the doors then re-open It, this god forsaken place would have disappeared."

They try what Will said but couldn't of been more wrong, the only change is one of the asylum corridor ceiling light has started flickering. I guess they will never know if they went when Will first said, they could have been safe but doesn't matter now, as they start to venture into the asylum.

The girls hiding behind the guys that call out for anyone to explain what is going on, but not a single-being calls back. Looking at the half hanging wallpapers thinking a lighters flame will have this place go up in flames. They look back just to see double doors that are locked by a chain with a number padlock dangling in the middle. So they start to look into the rooms, but only see bunkbeds with people most probably patients of this asylum. While Will rummages around in his bag, he pulls out a flashlight clicking it on, leaving his bag behind. He marches to the front, while the guys try the doors but they are all locked, he shines his light in through the wired mesh window, in the middle of the left side door, all he sees is a small crappy kitchen, that has a pot with baked beans within on the stove burning away, flames cracking onto the saucepans bottom like whipping some lady's ass.

Hearing people moaning in a sexual way, he goes to the other door on the right, peeping through seeing a doctor standing as bold as brass, while the nurse is on her knees, well I am sure I don't need to tell you, as they are not looking for his stethoscope, for the people who can't guess they are playing hide the sausage In her mouth mate. Will calls the others over, that all rush over to see what the door is concealing.

The girls say "Ew that is disgusting."

Donald is soon there recording with his camcorder.

While Cameron says "Go on my son, she is getting one of her five a day, his banana."

Will laughs uncontrollably before composing himself.

Teresa says "Yes, I remember reading about this fire last night, Sam was part of the firefighters that stopped this building burning down, killing the hundred patience."

Will responds saying "I bet this bit was kept out of their statements."

Donald says "All I know is I can't be the only one that has a semi, because of the nurse, her tits are so nice, perky, nipples the right size not cookie or coffee stain nips. That old wrinkly doctor is defiantly punching above his..."

Before Donald can finish what he is saying, Cameron quickly buts in by asking, "Where is your tape measure?"

Their expression quickly change from about to laugh to oh shit! As the window in the door behind them explodes outwards from a fire that has erupted inside. This must of woken up some of the crazies because like brainless zombies, they have started smacking on the double door windows, some rubbing their feces over the window, while screaming crazily along with some making weird laughing noises at the fire, like cavemen discovering fire for the first time. Fire spreading around the walls, catching on to the next piece of peeling wallpaper. As the student back off.

The whole room shape-shifts, to more of the corridor on fire, thick smoke everywhere but the students not feeling any effects, they back up to the door they come through,

Will picking up his bag. The chained double doors that the students are standing in front of, is getting bashed in by the firefighters, they are soon quick to move out of the way, as an axe with a few hits from the other side slices through chain, that slides out from the handle, clanking onto the ground below. As the firefighters burst through the double doors. The smoke is escaping as one of the firefighter carrying the hose sprays water all across the walls to doors, another firefighter behind guiding the pipe through making sure It doesn't get twisted or stuck slowly progressing through the corridor. As the students escape through the bashed in double doors, to another part of the mental asylum corridor, finding a stairway, that they walk down.

They get to the bottom of the stairs, Will just managed to grab ahold of his bag, in their escape.

Teresa says "That was so weird, we was there but it was like we wasn't there."

Angela responds saying "I know what you mean, one of the firefighters looked at me but it was like he looked straight through me."

Cameron says "Maybe it was Sam, we can find a way out through this door."

They look through the doors window just to see more asylum corridor.

Will with his flashlight opens the door, everyone walks through following Will, seeing the morning break through the curtains, they find themselves standing in someone's living room. The whole house seems as it's sleeping, no movement until behind the television that is in the corner of the room, a dual plug-socket sparks bursting into flames, the students panic Donald runs through a doorway into the kitchen, after a few seconds of hearing running water, he comes back with a full of water dark grey sink washing-up bowl, just about to throw it on to the source of the fire.

Will stops him while he says asking "Are you fucking stupid? Water onto electricity doesn't mix very well, you will get us all killed or yourself."

The fire now speeding up the curtains to engulfing the whole of the wall, to the ceiling, blistering the paint off from the walls. The lightbulb explodes along with the fabric of the lampshade burning to a crisp. Will throws the water at the burning wall but it does nothing, the fire alarm is sounding. A young lad runs down the stairs in his boxers to witness the blaze at full effects.

Angela shouts "Wait!"

But the lad doesn't hear her, he runs back up stairs screaming in terror.

The room shape-shifts to the ceiling collapsing through, the extinguished room dripping with water, they extinguished the room with water, after brought in a type C extinguisher to put the fire out at its source. It seems like the students are glued to the spot. The people that live inside the house are evacuated, well that is what they think, the mother asking where her other son is.

The fire marshal shouts "Sam, get fucking back here! it's too dangerous!"

They watch as Sam the fireman runs up into the houses, up the stairs he goes, with his red handled axe. The students allowed to move, of course they head for the front door, joining the people outside but not a single soul acknowledging them, Will clutching his bag.

They're waving in people's faces but doesn't make any difference. Sam re-emerges from the soaked burnt house, you can see through one of the pipes that is loops into his breathing apparatus witch is aiding the boy with breathing , part of the stairs collapsing. Sam sweating walking towards the bystanders, a handsome man the ladies would say, with dark facial features, he has the mother's son over his shoulder, muffled coughing from the boy as Sam delivers him to her, she hugs her son, while hugging Sam, she says "Thank you" multiple times.

The students smiling at the kindest gesture any person could do, which is to save another humans life. As the paramedics take Sam's breathing mask off the boys face, to put their one on him to get all the smoke out from his young lungs. The homes bath slides out of the upstairs bathroom into the soaking burn rubble below, but Cleveland isn't having a bath this time, everyone stepping back avoiding any flying debris.

Teresa says "I remember reading about this one as well last night."

Cameron responds saying "Yeah, I remember watching the news when I was a kid, this happened ages ago, he risked his life to save the boy."

Suddenly the surrounding neighborhood starts collapsing even the people they melt into the ground.

Around the students a hotel room rises, the first thing you will notice is the glare of the television, which is lighting up the half asleep man, laying on top of the bed sheets, fully dressed just without his footwear which are tucked under the dressing table. A half smoking cigarette between his fingers, with the window open, the fire alarm hanging off from the ceiling, disarmed. The man dozes off, the students are quick to try the hotel room door. Cameron nearly falls backwards because he forcefully opens the hotel door, they are all quickly rushing out to the hotels hallway, doors along both sides. They frantically try all the doors until....

Will calls out "Over here guys!"

The other four come rushing over to him into the pitch black room, the door shuts behind them.

Angela finds the light switch after patting the wall near the doorframe a few times, flicking the switch on really dim lights Startling the students with a couple having wild passionate sex on the bed, with flickering candles on all the other surfaces. The attractive woman is riding him, moaning along with kissing each other's body parts. At any second their night of passion could go up in flames, bedsheets along with pillows all over the show, lack of concentration, the fabric is very flammable to burning candles.

In a blink of their eyes the room shape-shifts to the hotels kitchen downstairs, the students stand at the pass while the chef flips the food within the pan by shaking it, fire blazing up with every shake. While the couple of chefs around are working, the students stand watching from the pass, one of the chef in his whites, pulls two plates out from the hot draw, as the other chef with yellow handle tongs picks the steak up from one of the other pans, putting it on a tray to rest for a minute.

Cameron asks "Teresa did you read about this one?"

Teresa responds saying "Yes I did but this fire didn't start in any of the places we have been shown."

The chefs have put the two dishes together, with beautiful presentation. One of the chefs with a bit of blue tissue wipes around the edge of the plate, as the other dings the bell, after taking the next order from the machine, calling out the ticket

"Listen! Bouche for two, after one small Caesar salad, no anchovies, sauce on the side chef, one bruschetta caprese, mains after.

The other chefs responds shouting "Yes chef!"

After he puts it up in the ticket holder.

Teresa says "I wish I could remember how this one started."

Angela says "I remember."

As she turns to leave, a waiter coming to collect the food walks through Angela, she looks puzzled but continues to leave the kitchen to go in the hotels lobby....

The rest are in hot pursuit walking down a small corridor, she goes up to white closed double doors, when she opens both doors a backdraft of fire happens, but the flames don't scorch their skin. The flickering flames being blocked by the spirit of Sam, with half burnt on fire gear that is melted into his skin. With his back to the students that back out of the way, while flames whipping around him at them, like a angry person being held back, lashing out. The flames inside the room die down, the receptionist nearly falls off her chair, as she quickly grabs the landline to call the fire department.

Sams turns facing them with his muffled voice because of his breathing apparatus melted into his face "Can't let the fire have all the fun, revenge is a dish best served cold."

In a blink of their eyes, Sam has disappeared along with their surroundings....

They are standing in the original house, standing on the stairs, the guys on one side, on the other stair case are the ladies. A knock on the door echoing through the whole homes frame. The students rush down the stairs, hoping it is the old bill or some kind of authority so they quickly open the door. Samantha stands there with a massive grin on her face.

She says "Oh hello, you must be the students that Gonzalo, our groundskeeper said was coming. I am Samantha, nice to meet you."

She goes to shake their hands but instead they start panicky, frantically explaining what they have been experiencing. By this time Samantha has walked in to the house, along with started to walk through the dining room, a nice room by the way you know a fancy one, with a big dark wood dining room table, you know I come from a council estate flat so didn't have a dining room. Anyway I digress from this story so let's get back to it, Samantha walks through the dining room into the kitchen.

Teresa furiously asks "Are you even fucking listening?"

Samantha responds saying "You sound like the previous woman of the house, this place isn't haunted it's too much of a beautiful house to be."

Samantha fills up the kettle while Donald is rummaging in Wills bag to bring out the camcorder, oh yeah he put his camcorder in Will's bag, when they were stuck in the flaming house that Sam saved that boy from. He is showing her the footage that was captured, on the small screen you can see when the students first walk in to the mansion. Donald splitting off from the group walking through the dining room into the kitchen, filming around everything. The reflection of Sams face, with the breathing apparatus melting into his face, pure anguish as this happens in the window, but at that time Donald doesn't see this as he zooms through the kitchen window to the back-garden, an old tire is hanging from a big trees branch, where kids used to play....

The video shape-shifts before their very eyes, it goes to the groundskeeper Gonzalo cutting the grass with a green lawnmower, his two children swinging on the trees tire.

Donald says "That didn't happen before, I am sure I would remember that happening."

The screen flashes with the image of Gonzalo dead, blood seeping from the axe wound sticking out from head.

Will says "Fuck this, I am gone mate."

He rushes out of the kitchen, through the dining room to the front door, the others shortly following behind him, as Will opens the door, to that fatal night in Sam's life, as he lays asleep on the fire departments tattered sofa. Before they walk through but get rushed to, as Will looks back to Donald being strangled with hose by melted Sam, along with Samantha her hand over Donald's mouth while stabbing into his neck, severing his jugular blood pissing out. The girls screaming in terror while Cameron alongside Will are grabbing ahold of them, to get them away from harms way through the door, Will while trying to grab ahold of the doors handle, watching Donald suffocating with the hose wrapped around his throat, with blood spurting out. He shits himself shutting the door.

The door in a blink of their eyes disappears, just an old raggedy wall in front of them. Will starts punching into it while angrily saying "Fuck! Fuck! Fuck!"

With each punch his knuckles, skin tearing, blood seeping into the grazes to skin tearing on his middle finger knuckle, blood smearing on the wall along with over his knuckles on the last punch.

Angela asks "What the hell was that?"

Teresa responds saying "It is a placebo, they are not real, well she might be, but melted Sam isn't real."

Cameron responds saying angrily "No! You want to say that to Donald because it sure looked like he was fucking dying."

Will says asking "I don't know what they want, we must have to work this shit out. What do you remember about all of this case, that you read about last night?"

Teresa responds saying "That they believed it was arson but no one got charged, he was the only one that was in the building at the time, as we can see now he could have been asleep...."

Before she can say anymore a flaming Molotov, exploding through the small window, shards of glass explode into the room, as the lit Molotov catches the wrecked old curtains as it passes through exploding on to the carpet, fire spreads everywhere. The students are still anti-flammable but Sam isn't, flames are soon burning to melting everything in its path, Sam doesn't wake up in time to put a stop the fire spreading, like soft butter on bread. Something is seen because Will walks up to the broken window, smoke exhaling from, like a chimney on a old steam train. He peaks through to the cold of the evening, a figure leaning up against under a lamppost dressed all in black, with their hood up, my guess is that person is the one who done it. Vision is smoke full, Sam coughing choking on the smoke, screaming in anguish as the flames scorch his skin, arm hair burning, spreading up his arms catching on to his t'shirts sleeves. Sam getting up while he tries patting the spreading flames out while rushing over to the door. He tries to open the door but the door handle comes off in his hand, he stumbles backwards, falling hitting his head on the football tables edge, knocking himself out. The frame of the old building starts to collapse on its self.

The room is quick to shape-shift to the students standing outside, beside the fire marshal from the town their from, as the fire firefighters have arrived on scene, putting the rubble of fire, out. Luckily in the dead of the morning opposite the fire station, Mr Octahedral's weak bladder caused him to get up to go for a piss, a little peak outside which alerted him to the flames whipping out from the broken-in window of the fire station.

The extinguished pile of steaming rubble lay in front of the students, as passersby start to form a group at the cornered off police blue tape, asking the same kind of questions, "What happened?" "How did this happen?" "Was anybody inside?"

The police officers keeping guard around the steaming pile, can't answer any of their questions. As the firemen with fire women I am not sexist, just the sexiest. Anyway they are sieving through the rubble to find Sams body. Will noticing something out from the corner of his eye.

He asks "Cameron, isn't that your older brother?"

Will points him out in the crowd behind the old bills blue tape.

Cameron responds saying "Yes it is, I wonder what he was doing here, I know he used to work in this town but the other side, in the butchers."

Teresa responds saying "Maybe this was his route to work."

Cameron responds saying "No his route was different way, I remember dad dropping him off on his first day, he defiantly knows something."

One of the firemen shouting alerts the students to walk towards the rubble, the police officers not stopping them because like my nan, used to tell me when I was little kids should be seen but not heard, but it is really because they are being shown events, that have already been unraveled.

A fireman shouts "We can see a foot!"

To the fire marshal, that is speaking with the coroner, that has a black body bag in hand.

While walking towards the edge of the rubble, the fire marshal responds saying "Ok, be careful we need to preserve as much of his body as possible."

They're carefully removing burnt pieces of wood along melted objects until they are able to carefully lift Sams burnt body out.

Their surroundings shape-shifts to the morgue. Mr Preserve is showing Samantha, Sams body for the first time. The four students notice something that, I didn't portray the first time around, Sam in ghost form, wearing the same clothes he was burnt alive in, is standing behind Samantha, his arms around her waist. Sam notices the students as he lets go of Samantha, walking over to the four of them.

Sam says asking "There is meant to be five, Where is the other guy?"

Will responds asking "You killed him you dickhead, why did you send for us?"

Sam responds saying "No, that was the evil side of me, the bitter one for having to die prematurely. Before we put an end to this, I have to show you this."

Sam walks over Samantha which is crying, as she is hugging his lifeless body, kissing her on the forehead. After twirling his finger, as their surroundings shape-shifts again to...

Off we all go to Sams wake, he lays in the middle of the room, closed coffin. While Sam walks over towards the coffin closely followed by the students, people which were friends of Sams are speaking to each other, men dressed in black suits, the ladies dressed in black attire. Sams friends completely oblivious that they are even there as Sam's placing his hand on shoulders of his friends while maneuvering around the people.

He keeps saying "Thank you for coming out."

But no one can hear him but maybe in their own way they feel his presence. Arriving at his coffin where Samantha receiving condolences, shaking hands with the sad folks in mourning.

Cameron asks Sam "Do you know why my brother was at the scene where you died?"

Sam responds saying "Yes I do know, your brother used to play this game with an other guy that he worked with in the butchers, daring each-other to do stupid things."

Cameron in complete disbelief asks "So my brother dared his fucking mate to kill someone?"

Sam rubbing Samantha's arm, trying to comfort her but can't because he is a spirit.

He responds saying "Not like that, it was a dare that went south, your brother made the Molotov, his mate lit it to throw it through the window, he done it under the impression that I or no one else was in the fire department at night."

Cameron responds saying "I don't believe you, not my brother."

Sam responds asking "Why would you think I would fucking lie, when you die, you see the moments that lead to your death."

He takes a deep breath to calm himself down, funny really considering he's a spirit.

After he continues to tell Cameron "Listen I have forgiven their actions, but if you don't believe me, one of his friends died shortly after."

Cameron nods his head implying yes.

Sam continues to say "It was fire related, I tried to stop him from doing it, but I did stop him from ending your brothers life."

Cameron responds saying "I will end him, no one will touch or kill my brother."

Sam chuckles to himself after says "Be careful what you wish for, let's go because I am going to end this shit now, so I can enjoy the preserved memories with my beautiful lady, in the after life."

He pecks Samantha in the lips before walking away towards a doorway, she touches her lips like she felt it, the students follow Sam through the doorway....

Their surroundings change back to the mansion, but no sign of anybody, not even Donald, just a pool of blood on the marble floor.

Sam shouts out "Come on you fucker, come take this beating like a man!"

In a blink of an eye melted Sam is standing in front of them. He is quick to throw a punch at Sam, that can't do anything apart from take it on the chin, the two of them start fighting. While Sam stumbles back a little, Cameron punches bitter Sam square in his face but his fist, is just sucked through, like an female asshole. It only pisses off the evil Sam even more than he already is, which is near on impossible.

Sam says "Oh yeah I forgot to tell you, it won't hurt him at all if you hit him, he is a placebo. But thanks for trying."

Cameron responds saying "It was more for my brothers friend."

By this time the red fireman axe has appeared in the bitter Sams right hand, he swings it at Sam as the others back away, the girls run into the living room to hide. But are confronted by Samantha, that slashes through the air at them with a knife. Sam is quick to protect all the students by twirling his finger, sending them off to..., while he stays to fight the bitter twisted side of himself.

Cameron's brother is laying down on a hotel rooms bed, with curtains closed. He seems fidgety in his sleep, one thing which is strange if you look closely around the hotel room, which looks pretty standard, but you will all see the sockets have tape over them, even the television is laid down, unplugged, windows closed with the cream curtains tucked onto the window ledge, instead of draped over the white radiator. Now you may not think this is essential stuff to know but it is valuable knowledge. He is still sleeping, fidgeting while kicking the covers off from him, as the pillow beside him is levitating after goes to suffocate Cameron's brother. As the spiteful Sam starts to appear, holding the pillow but is quickly disrupted by good Sam barging from behind into him. They both tussle over the hotel bed, before they hit the floor, disappearing in falling mid-air, as Cameron's brother still lay In his disturbed sleep.

Going into his dream, Cameron's brother walking down a pathway, pulling his phone out from his pocket, before he clicks it on, fire combustion but instead in a state of panic dropping it to the floor or throwing It away, he puts his fire phone back into his pocket, maybe to show he isn't scared but it extinguishes itself while entering. As his surroundings become clearer, he looks to his right, a guy dressed all in black even his gloves are, with black sun glasses on, hood up with a cap on, a black bandanna covering the rest of his face. Cameron's brother looks down he is dressed the same, the customers along with checkout ladies stop what they are doing, putting their hands up, with a look of panic on their faces. The guy beside goes pointing the homemade machete, while walking towards the cashier.

He is aggressively shouting "Everyone shut the fuck up! Empty the tills!"

Cameron's brother springs into action as he walks towards the same cashier, cricket bat in hand, in his other a black bin bag, he gives it to the middle aged woman.

Cameron's brother in the same manner of tone as his friend said, says "Fucking fill it up!"

She shakes her head in a no motion, words not wanting to leave her mouth because of fear, but at the same time maybe afraid of losing her job. He leans closer towards her, to the point she can most probably feeling his faint breath, a reflection on his sun glasses is of her. He pulls down his own bandanna, showing the bottom half of his face, her eyes glued to his mouth.

Cameron's brother calmly says "I was hoping you would say that, so I had a reason, thank you."

He jabs a guy with the cricket bat, that was waiting in line, wallet in hand to buy the stuff he needs. Braking his nose dropping his wallet to the floor, while stumbling backwards. Tears starts rolling down her cheeks as she opens the tills, emptying out all of the money.

The other robber asks in a polite manner "Where is your manager? I have a little bone to pick my dear."

One of the cashiers, nervously points towards white swinging double doors, to the side beside the crisps isle.

The guy says "Thank you madam, just saved yourself a bloody nose."

He goes towards the double doors, pulling out a black bag from his pocket.

The robber is walking down a corridor towards a brown door at the end, kicking it in.

A males voice shouts out "I told no one to disturb us, while I train Cindy."

A guy is leaning back on the desk, with trousers around his ankles, getting his dick sucked by who I would presume is Cindy.

The robber says "Well, that is one way to be teachers pet, I am here to unload the money from the safe."

The manger pushes Cindy's head back, after picks up his trousers.

Cindy still on her knees complaining asking "What about my pay rise?"

The manager quickly rushes over to the Safe behind the desk, opening to filling, while the robber steps into the room, helping Cindy up by her arm, after walks her over to the manager, passing him the black bag, while he is filing it up.

The robber says to Cindy "Maybe we can help each other, give me a raise down below, when I want it, I am sure I can do the same for you, little gold digging slut."

She just giggles while latching on to him, like a baby suckling from their mums tit. The manager passes Cameron's brothers mate the black bag filled with money. He shoves Cindy away after *WHACK* smashing the managers head off from the desk, knocking him out, just in case he calls for help.

A couple of seconds later, Cameron's brother is walking down the same corridor towards the door that is slightly open, he seems in a rush, checking over his shoulder with every step, with the black bag filled with cash from the registers over his shoulder, barging the back door open. Nothing could of prepared him for what he was going to see, which is his mate in the same position as the manager earlier, but the manager is laying spark'o on the ground. Cindy has a sure talent for getting raises.

Cameron's brother just loudly laughs "Come on, old bill is on their way I can hear sirens."

As his mate is doing his jeans up, while Cindy gets off her knees, with her index finger she is wiping the edge of her lips.

His mate says "I was trying to, on her tits bro."

After he grabs the safes money black bag, as he leaves the room to catch up with Cameron's brother that is near the back door, with Cindy following closely behind his mate, as they get to the back door, pushing it open.

Instead of Cameron's brother standing in a car park or some sort of behind the shop area surrounded by big bins. Nah he is at his old job, inside the butchers with blue latex gloves on, knife in hand with a slab of beef on a red board, he is cutting them into steaks. Over his shoulder through a doorway, is the owner of the butchers, wearing butchers attire, speaking with a customer. The red handled knife slicing through the meat like a warm knife with butter, spreading, melting into toast. Cameron's brothers mate comes through the heavy set white door, closing it behind him, walking up to stand beside Cameron's brother.

He says "Just brought some new trainers, with the money we robbed then got a blowy from that Cindy slag mate."

Cameron's brother responds saying "Yeah aright, keep it down, don't want him to hear out there."

Putting the blade down after placing the steaks into grey polystyrene trays, to cover with cling film, pricing after sell them to the public.

His mate responds saying "Fuck him, I'll carve him a new arsehole with my machete."

Cameron's brother responds saying "Alright fucking Texas chainsaw, well in your case machete massacre."

As he is chuckling out loud, he can hear from behind him the owner of the butchers asking "Hello Officer, what can I do for you?"

He turns around to see the two police officer speaking with the owner, after looking to his left to see his mate has already scarpered.

The remaining students are plonked into a forest, their eyes are quick to lash from one side to another, to familiarize themselves to their surroundings. But all they see are trees, along with the earths dirt.

Besides the wind whistling through the trees like an old pirate whistling a shanty tune on his ships deck.

Will breaks the silence saying asking, "That was rather nice of Sam to send us to the middle of bum fuck no where, what do we do now?"

Cameron responds saying "Bro be grateful he saved us, could of easily been killed off back there."

Teresa adds her two pence in "Yeah, plus didn't see you doing anything."

Will responds saying "Fuck that mate, if his evil side didn't think twice about punching himself in the face, he certainly won't for me."

Teresa responds saying "Exactly, so be grateful anyway I think he is still testing us, we need to look around."

So twigs start snapping under their shoes as they walk deeper into the forest, trainer prints squished into the mud, that it seemed to have been rained on recently.

Cameron's brother alongside his mate, are unloading a frozen pigs carcass off from the back of the local farms truck. Both wearing correct safety attire, as they are carrying the carcass one at each side, taking it through the back door of the butchers, towards the walk-in freezer, where they will hang it up to use at a later time. Cold frost departing from the freezer doorway, like steam rising from a hot cup of tea. The freezer sits adjacent to the walk-in fridge, that is beside the preparation area of all the meat. The lads walk in to the freezer, hanging the carcass on hooks in the middles, beside the other frozen animal carcasses.

His mate says "The shop we robbed has got cameras inside now."

Cameron's brother says "Mate, why don't you run an television advert telling people what we done, keep it down would you."

Cameron's brother looks around from the freezers doorway, to check where the owner is but it is fine he is speaking with the farmer.

His mate says "Don't worry if he hears, we will just tell him we are playing a video game."

Cameron's brother responds asking "Okay, how you know that they got cameras."

His mate says "Cindy told me."

Cameron's brother responds asking "For fuck sake your not still banging that are you? Also how does she know? I fucking hope she hasn't gone back there to work."

His mate responds saying "Err, yeah a score for a score mate, sometimes we go twice or three times, don't worry she hasn't but her mum told her."

Hearing the back door close, they both walk out from the walk-in freezer.

Cameron's brother says to his friend "We will speak about this later."

The owner of the butchers asks "Tommy, can you make some minced beef please, seven trays should do it mate."

Cameron's brother Tommy "Sure, Derek."

Derek responds says "Thanks mate, now you."

He points to Tommy's mate, now Derek isn't his biggest fan if it wasn't for Tommy, covering his ass along with sticking up for him, he would have been gone a long time ago.

Derek carries on demanding "Scott, clean up this place, this is a butchers not a fucking pig sty boy."

As he is angrily saying this, Scott can't help but smirk noticing his chins wave like you've just seen a friend across the road, as Derek furiously shakes his head.

The rest of the students are treading carefully through the forest, while keeping their eyes peeled for anything that will be of significance. A shuffling of leaves grab their attention quickly, but it is a measly black bird, picking a twig up for her nest. They come to a clearing with-in the forest, to a deep stream but the water is so clear you can see the beautiful stone bottom, with many trouts alongside salmon swimming around. A multi-coloured dragonfly is in-flight through the middle of the stream.

Will asks "Teresa, do you remember anything about a forest, when you was doing research last night?"

Before Teresa can respond, Angela starts tearing up as one is striding down her cheek, she is trying to hold them back, but can't bursting into tears, the others are confused at why she is crying, so they comfort her until her tears are gone.

Angela still whimpering says "I know what happened, I have spent many days in these woods before I knew you guys, trying to contact my father, see the last city's fire was in this forest, my father was apart of the few that didn't make it out."

Cameron says "Don't be sad, all them times you tried to contact your father wasn't a waste because you will be able to see him again."

Cameron wipes away her tears with his index finger, that was rolling down her blushing cheeks.

Will asks "Do you two need a moment?"

Cameron asks "Would you?"

Will responds saying "I would."

He walks away with Teresa, while muttering under his breath to Teresa "That was a bit intense, thought he was going to, you know fuck her against the tree or something, Jesus mate."

They carry on walking through the stream to the other side, to give the other two some privacy.

Tommy is washing his hands in a hand washing sink at work, the day is nearly complete, Derek comes out from the office, with two envelopes in hand. Scott has finished early most probably fooling around with that Cindy chick.

While Tommy is drying his hand with blue tissues, Derek is walking up to him while whistling, Derek hands him both envelopes.

He says "Enjoy your weekend son, see you Monday."

Tommy responds saying "Yeah, thank you Derek, enjoy yours as well."

Derek shakes Tommy's hand after walks back to his office, while Tommy looks down at the chunky envelopes, spreading them out, his name on one, Scott is handwritten on the other envelope. Tommy knowing what they are, finished for the week, he puts the envelopes in his back pocket after goes to the changing room to get changed.

The passenger side black saloon car door opens, from within by Scott, Tommy getting in greeted by Scott in the drivers seat. Looking over his shoulder Cindy is sitting in the middle of the back seats. Cindy goes to say something but Tommy cuts her off saying....

"She isn't coming mate, better drop her off home."

Scott responds saying "Yeah you right, just thought she could be...."

Tommy cuts in again saying "At home, that is where she will be."

Scott looks at Cindy saying "Sorry babe."

Tommy asks him "What have you told her?"

Scott responds saying "Nothing mate, just we was going on a drive."

Tommy responds saying "Okay, keep it that way."

Tommy fiddles around his bag for a second while Scott starts his car up, pulling out from the parking space as Tommy places the one that doesn't have his name on envelope onto Scott's lap.

Let's go see what the students are up to my friend, Will is with Teresa still, they have found a dusty path that leads through the forest.

Will calls back to the other two "Come on, when we make it out of here, you two can have your romance."

The other two jog up to Will alongside Teresa.

Cameron says asking "You haven't got a heart, what have you guys found?"

Will responds saying "Not when I am trapped in a fucking nightmare, that I am trying to get us out from mate. We have found a path, if you look close enough there is an edge of a building."

Angela says "I don't have a good feeling about this."

Will says "Same, but could be our way out, fifty - fifty chance, so let's go check it out."

They carry on walking down the path.

Let's go have a butchers at Tommy my friend, he Is still in the car with Scott, they are dropping Cindy off at her house.

Before she leaves Cindy asks "When will I see you next?"

Scott responds saying "I will contact you."

Cindy gets out from the car, Scott is quick to pull away. Before anything else can happen, the surroundings around Tommy, melt away even Scott, face to his body, like a freshly painted canvas that has had a water chucked over it.

Tommy abruptly wakes from his dream, panting as he has just re-lived apart from his life, that maybe he would like to of forgotten. Pillow soaked from his perspiration, he wipes his forehead with a tissue from the bedside table.

Tommy groans as he gets out from the bed. Making his way to the bathroom, stretching on his way. He pulls the string to turn the light on with flickers before it stops, walking up to the sink with the mirror ahead of him. Putting the plug in its rightful place, filling up the sink, with both taps. Stopping the taps just before It overflows down the little hole. Cupping his hands he splashes the water over his face, twice after looks in to the mirror, before I can describe how he looks but, I can tell you he looks like a man that needed that sleep because, he hasn't for a few days, evil Sam stands behind burnt half face grinning. The good Sam comes from the side, punching his evil self after they both disappear. Tommy in a state of panic quickly turns around, droplets of water dripping off his face, grabbing a hotel towel to dry his face.

Back to the remaining students that have made their way, to the building at the end of the path to a log cabin hotel deep in the woods.

Will asks "Angela, how did your father die?"

Angela responds saying "My mum just said in a fire, in these woods."

Cameron opens the hotel doors for the others to walk through.

Teresa asks "Was your mum with him when it happened?"

Angela responds saying "Not sure, all I know is she was pregnant with me at the time, she said when he died she was lucky to fall in love again."

They are standing in the lobby of the cabin hotel, at the tidy reception, sitting behind is a smartly dressed heavy set woman, which is sorting out some papers, a woman is being led away, joyfully towards some stairs, their finger inter-locked, with giggles coming from both of them like a naughty juvenile couple.

Will says "That could be your parents."

Angela says "From behind that looks like my mother but If it is, she isn't with my father, he is...."

She points to a man, in the waiting area reading the paper, well more spying as he is folding the left corner of the newspaper, heartbreak in his eyes.

Angela responds saying "I remember reading about this one, they didn't rip it down or re-build, just an empty burnt out log cabin hotel."

Teresa nods her head, the couple are halfway up the stairs, as Angela's father gets up from the seat to follow, but before he does, he goes over to the reception lady. Who glances up then back down to what she is doing. Angela's father coughs to grab the reception lady's attention.

She asks "Can I help you, sir?"

He responds asking "Yes, a weird request. Can I have a room next to that couple, that just passed through please? See I can't sleep if I am not beside other people in the next room, you wouldn't want me coming down here, walking around all night long."

She responds saying "No, we wouldn't want that now sir, I bet your wife loves you."

Clearly seeing his wedding band on his finger that he keeps twisting, nervously.

He responds saying "Yeah, you would think she does."

She responds saying "Okay, room thirty seven is ready, that will be a hundred pound for the night please,

buffet breakfast in the morning til ten, half eleven is checkout time."

She hands him a form to fill out with a pen she places on top, he Is quick to fill it out as his Impatience is growing, as every second passes. The ink is quickly scribbling down his personal information. Angela just a arms length away from her father, a man she never met, her eyes welling up, wishing that she could touch, hug, even just to speak to him, she goes to speak but nothing comes out. As her father checks out that everything Is written on the form, checking the other side, but nothing for him to fill out.

He says "Done."

While she takes the paper giving it a check over, he pulls his wallet out to pay, counting the money, after placing five twenties on the side, the receptionist places the paper down, after grabs the money like a hungry hippo grabbing its food, counting it after places it in the till, but pockets twenty quid in the process. Angela's father starts tapping his fingers while the receptionist is fiddling around in the desks draw, pulling out his rooms key, he snatches it from her hand , in a rush while he storms towards the stairs to his room.

He says "Thank you."

The receptionist responds saying "Your welcome sir."

Angela is quick to follow after her father. But she doesn't get far before everything in their surroundings start to turn to ashes, without fire, floating through the air, pieces of the receptionist like confetti being thrown at a wedding. To the carpet, strands of fabric float path the students eyes like a worm across muddy ground. Shards of curtain blowing through the air, like leaves leaving trees.

Their surroundings building back up, quicker than you can imagine, every bit of material fitting in to place, perfectly. They stand at the side of a bed, being mysteriously constructed in front of their eyes, a couple laying, on top kissing passionately. Angela realizes that it is her mother pregnant with her, clearly cheating on her father. The couple start stripping off, chucking their clothes everywhere behind them, not a care in the world, like horny teenagers, groans coming from the couple, kissing each others necks, nibbling on her ear, biting his lip as she is undoing his belt buckle. Kissing his neck leading to his chest, he kicks his jeans after boxers off, she gives him a hand, if you know what I mean. Angela notices from the corner of her eye, you can see into the next room, all you can see from wall is the cement outlines. Angela fathers pressed against the wall, his ear to a glass, listening in to his pregnant wife riding some next man. They both start wildly moaning, as she rides faster, playing with her milk-filled boobs. A tear streams down Angela's fathers cheek, which has the same effect on Angela, seeing her father cry.

Tommy is rushing down a different hotel stairs, skipping steps in the process of trying to get his jacket on, laces not even tied up properly. Dashing past the hotel reception, placing his hotel room keys on the side in the process, the elderly guy on the reception asks "Did you enjoy your stay, sir?"
Tommy sarcastically responds "Yes, it was lovely."
He shuts the heavy wooden door behind him.

Tommy makes it to his car that's parked up within the hotels car park, that he quickly gets into, starting her engine he is quick to leave, tires pushing the gravel away as he turns the car out of its parking space. He drives onto the main road, lucky for him no traffic, as he clearly seems to be in a rush. Driving past a park, as he deeply inhales to calm himself down, at seeing the person he can only presume, is the one he played a hand in killing, but not meaning to. Exhaling, he does this a few more times, getting himself calm again. He starts fiddling around his car CD player. He doesn't see what he is driving into, until he smashes into the desk, after the wall from that fatal night, his airbag explodes on impact as he shakes around, bashing into the back of his seat then Into the airbag but doesn't stop Tommy from being knocked out. His surroundings are the fire station mess room with Sam still alive, sleeping on the couch.

Do you wonder what my students are up to? Yes so do I, let's go have a watch. Angela coughing from the thick dark smoke, looking around frantically trying to see the others, while calling their names, no one calls back. Flames spreading up the side of the wall in front of her, putting her hands over her mouth, crouching down to find a way out from the hotel room, seeing some legs run past In front of her to a door that swings open, clattering into the desk behind smoke escaping, she follows like the smoke in hot pursuit, on all fours, like a dog. Fire alarms blaring out, along with sirens wailing in the distance, getting closer with every mili-second, that is currently passing. Angela makes it out of the door, flickering flames whipping above her, she goes to crouching to standing, smoke filling every inch of space above, seeing someone what looks like her mother, running away to get her along with her baby out from danger. The building starts falling down, chunks of ceiling. The door to the hotel room that Angela's fathers in opens, he steps out coughing, his cheating wife not to faraway, looks back to see him right before a chunk of ceiling followed by a beam, crushing him but not killing him. She squints wondering who it is, she can't stop as she is being lead away to safety.

Angela trying to lift the rubble of her crushed dying Dad, her face becoming more blackened by the fire, tears streaming down her cheeks, pushing the smoke dirt sideways with every tear stream. The smoke isn't affecting her anymore, she chucks a chunk of broken wood off the rubble. Her father coughing, spluttering blood, he takes his last breath as his eyes shut for good. She doesn't notice as she chucking rubble behind her, cutting her hands in the process, until good Sam pulls her back. She doesn't realize it's him, starts pummeling his chest, until he hugs her tightly.

Sam says "I am so sorry, you had to see that, but you had to know the truth."

She is hysterically crying while screaming "Why!?"

Sam says "I along with my brothers in arms, will be here soon to put this fire out. Listen I am going to get you to safety but at the moment I can't save your friends but I will."

He twirls his index finger around until they disappear.

Will is the first one bursting out from the hotel lobby doors, coughing along with gasping for air, followed by the other two, bent over in the same manner as Will. After they have caught their breath, Cameron looks around frantically, noticing Angela is not with them. Before he can ask where she is, Sam appears from out the edge of forest, walking across the path to greet them.

Sam says "Don't worry, Angela is safe she won't be continuing with you guys."

He looks from the students to the hotel, pointing towards something.

While continuing to tell "Listen, I am going to deal with you, leave them alone!"

Before they can ask anything he has disappeared. They notice no one has come out from the hotel along with sirens have stopped, also the alarm has stopped blaring out, they check what Sam was shouting out at, in anticipation. They turn looking at the log cabin hotel, that Is now decrepit, fire damaged, along with derelict, apart from evil Sam in one of the top windows, grinning at them as he puts the fireman axe over his shoulder, disappears in a blink of their eyes, the place is somewhat scary in its appearance.

While they decide what to do next, let's go see what Tommy is up to. Still laying unconscious slumped over his car steering wheel. His car crashed in the room that Sam was killed in. Let's take a little peak to see what his mind is playing. Tommy is standing beside Scott, both dressed in black, gloves on with masks on to cover their faces. This time round they have dared each other to rob a jeweler, Tommy is smashing the cases with all types of jewelry inside, Why Scott deals with the others inside the store. Tommy filling his bag, not even stopping to check what he is stealing, as long as they have carats, so they can flog it.

Tommy's surroundings shape-shifts to him standing at the cash register, serving an elderly lady a pack of sausages, along with minced beef, that she is putting inside a white carrier bag.

Tommy says "That will be seven pound please madam."

The lady while finder her purse from her handbag, responds saying "I haven't been called madam in a long while, my late husband Reginald called me that, when we started courting son, he was a butcher."

Tommy takes the ten pound note from the lady, sorting her change out with the cash register.

He responds saying "Nice to know madam, got to respect my elders after all I was raised by my grandparents."

The lady takes her change from Tommy's offering hand.

She responds saying "Wish there was more men like you."

Tommy smiles at her as she takes her bag from the side after putting it in her hand truck trolley.

As she says "Goodbye dear, see you next week."

Tommy responds saying "Goodbye madam, not if I see you first."

She chuckles to herself as she leaves the butchers.

Tommy cleaning the front of the butchers shop, which is free from customers. Scott has come in to start his shift. He shuffles over to Tommy, that is spraying disinfectant on the display window. Now the heat is off them for robbing the jewelry store, they stashed the jewelry in a secret place before laying low but luckily the old bills attention was soon turnt away from the robbery because a bank got robbed a few days after along with the security guards killed on sight. Oh how their families grieved, brung the community together shame it has to come to someone dying to do that, anyway back to this story. You see Tommy alongside Scott aren't bad people, they have their reasons why they dare each-other to do what they done, the thrill, the adrenaline given to them during an ordinary boring life, but they wouldn't intentionally kill anyone. Scott just about to ask something but Tommy cuts in.

Asking "You know the fire station in this town?

Scott nods that he does, Tommy wipes the display case.

While saying "I dare you to burn it down, It Is empty at night also there is no other building or homes attached."

Scott says "Okay, but when I have done it, you will have to do a dare."

Tommy agrees after says "I will make the Molotov, all you will have to do is light it after chuck it through the top window, you will do it tonight."

Suddenly before anything else can be said....

Tommy wakes up in his crashed car In the fire station before the fire happened, Sam still asleep on the rundown couch. Groggily lifting his head from the deflated airbag, looking around he realizes he is in unfamiliar surroundings. Broken pieces of wood from the desk laying over his car bonnet, Tommy checking that he can move, making sure nothing is broken along with him not being trapped, all is good considering. He pushes open his car door, that just thumps the ground, smashing the glass within. He steps out smashed glass under his trainers cracking some more, as he steps away from the wreckage.

He calls out asking "Buddy, you alright?"

Tommy goes over to shakes him....

Justin sitting inside his paddy wagon, the morning has just started to become more apparent. He is twiddling his thumbs waiting for something to happen until a lady's voice comes over his police radio...

Saying "We have a suspected missing persons for two nights, last seen on Friday by his mother, she called it in, apparently him along with four friends share a hobby, which is of the paranormal agenda, she told me they went to the old fire station residents, so best check there out first."

Justin picks up his corded walky-talky from its silver clip.

He asks "That Is the second one this year, has his mother tried to call him or the others?"

A few seconds pass before the woman speaks, answering "Yes, she has tried calling all of them on multiple times throughout Sunday, even contacted their parents, but their phones are off."

Justin responds saying "Okay I am gong there now, send for backup along with an ambulance team to meet me there please."

The lady responds asking "Okay, will do, what is your ETA?"

Justin while starting his police car up responds saying "Ten minutes."

Justin turns his steering wheel leaving from his stationary position.

The remaining students surroundings shape-shifts to them standing in a corridor of the fire station, pictures of the firefighting crew on the wall, along with moments they were tackling fires, spectacular pictures shot by the members of the public in these moments of destructive terror, leading up the stairs in front of them. While the students are looking at the different pictures, a thud comes from up the stairs, stopping them in their tracks.

Teresa says "We should go check that out."

Will responds saying "Fuck that, I have watched a lot of horror films, always a good way to get ourselves killed."

The other two not listening as they are walking deeper up the stairs.

Cameron says "There is three of us."

Will while having no choice but to follow, saying "Yeah, there was five mate."

They reach the top of the landing.

Tommy grunting while trying to pick up the sleeping Sam, with some strength, adrenaline along with knowing that time is running out. He manages to put Sam over his shoulder, struggling to stand straight, grunting in the process, he makes it to door, reaching out for the handle, the door bursts open, Tommy steps back luckily for himself or Sam not getting hit by the door in the process. The students standing in front of him, Tommy looking over their faces until his eyes clock Cameron.

Cameron says asking "Bro, what you doing here?"

Tommy struggling because of the lump of man on his shoulder, saying "Doing the right thing this time bro, help me get him out of the building, we don't have time."

The students sensing the urgency in his voice help him get sleeping Sam out from danger, they make it down the stairs to the door, Teresa opens. The lads get through the door without bumping Sams head off things on the way down to through, laying him on the cold concrete floor. Teresa looking up seeing, putting her hand flat up.

Teresa shouts "Stop!"

To Scott thats dresses in black, face covered along with black gloves throwing the flaming Molotov, that Tommy, made, Is flipping through the air as flames are growing down the rag towards the window, connecting with the glass as the flame meets the fuel, igniting. The students, Tommy along with Sam disappear into thin air.

Inside the fire station room moments before, Sam is standing alongside his evil side, Tommy's car still crashed inside.

Sam says "See it was an accident, given a second chance, he would of stopped it. So now rest within me so I can enjoy the timeless memories I have with Samantha."

The evil side of Sam turns to him, nods then steps disappearing inside as the Molotov smashes through the window, fire spreading everywhere, the room quickly on fire. Sam walks through the flickering flames, stepping over the car door, to his mess room door, leaving through it, closing the door behind him.

Justin arriving at the now house that is on the plot of land that the fire station was on, parking beside Wills car.

Grabbing his corded walky-talky saying "I am the first person here, I am going to go in."

The woman's voice responds saying "Wait for backup, ETA is two minutes."

Justin puts the walky-talky back, after gets out his cop car, looking at the house face on, all of the lights are off. Looking around he realizes he doesn't have his torch, grabbing his phone out, putting its light on, a ray streams out pointing It towards Wills car, but nothing, after he notices the groundskeepers, but again doesn't stop to look, he proceeds to the front door, with his shoulder, barging it open, he walks in.

Leaving the door open for his backup, shining his phones torch around.

He calls out asking "Hello, anybody home!?"

Eerie silence greets him back, the light shines on the puddle of blood, like a spotlight shining on a ballerina practice performing ballet on a stage to the empty red theater chairs, with the crowd coming later to watch, enjoying in silence.

Justin shouts out again anyone "It Is the police! I am not here to hurt you! Is there anyone here!?"

He points the light towards the living room doorway, Will comes frantically around the corner, towards him. Chills run over Justin, scarring him nearly Into next week. Poor Justin didn't know what to do, didn't know If he should throw a punch, give Will a hug or throw his phone at him.

Will panicky says "Please help us, they're just standing there in the corner."

Justin decides to follow through to the living room, Will trying to flick a light switch on in the process, but it doesn't come on. He walks beside Will into the living room, pointing the light around the room, stopping on Teresa, facing the corner, switching to the other corner, Cameron in the same position as Teresa.

A voice breaks the silence from behind, deeply shouting "Police! We are coming in!"

The ambulance lights flashing through the windows, as it is driving towards the house, sirens sounding.

The end....

Of course it isn't my friend, Samantha is walking down the corridor beside a nurse, that is working for the out of towns mental asylum.

All kind of weird noises along with screams, some eerie laughing coming from behind the corridor doors.

The nurse says "They was admitted here from the hospital, poor souls didn't stand a chance going into that house."

Samantha responds saying "I know, *tut* *tut.* Didn't stand a chance against my beautiful Sam."

The nurse looks at her confused while Samantha stabs her in the ribs twice while covering the nurses mouth, watching her life drain away, she closes her eyes,

Samantha pushing her back trying to guide her down so no screams can alert other people. The nurses body thumps into one of the many padded cell room door. Alerting the patient inside, noises from the lunatic wilding inside, the nurse slumps to the ground, with blood seeping out on to her clean pressed uniform, filling up her skirt, the more seeps until it spills out the sides, onto the cold laminated asylum floor. Samantha wipes the serrated blade on the nurses uniform, as she lay on the floor gasping for air, twitching. After Samantha puts her knife in her handbag while walking up to a room at the end, peering through the wire mesh window, seeing into the padded room, sits shaking Teresa in a straight jacket. Samantha looks into the room on her right, pacing the room in a straight jacket, while speaking to himself is Cameron. She goes to check the opposite room, looking through the window to see if Will is inside, straight jacketed up, but he is not just a empty cell, that is when she realizes the door is slightly open.

Samantha asking to herself "Where the fuck is the other one?"

She notices from the corner of her eye, a figure stands further up the corridor with his straight jacket in hand. I guess you could say when there is a Will, there is a way.

Gifted Hands

<u>A product of An Essence Of Time, so read that story before
reading this one please.</u>

<u>Now it's time for you to see, the curtains open up on my
cinema screen, salted or sweet popcorn at the ready, or maybe
you prefer a mixture of both, along with your fizzy drink,
comfortably enjoy. Have you been to the bathroom to spend a
penny? Don't want you to move from your seat until the visual
story is finished.</u>

A run down corridor Max is stumbling down, towards the
flat he lives in at the bottom, shabby wooden doors conceal
other peoples flats like Maxes. Burning this place down would
be a step to improvement. He stops halfway, half-cut, leaning
against the wall, taking a swig of whiskey from the bottle in
his right hand, like the plaster from these walls, it trickles
down. Max is half plastered, just like these walls, stumbling,
the noisy corridor starts to come to life in the distance, coming
from the right of the neighboring places. One of the flat
doors open to Max's right side, with a half dressed skinny
geezer being thrown out, crashing into the wall on impact,
knocking more of the walls contents off, crumbling to the
floorboards like this geezer trying to get up, as a larger than
life fella comes storming out from the flat, his scarred
tattooed fist connects with other guys jaw.

While he angrily says, spit flings out from his mouth,
"Fucking scummy cunt! sleeping with my woman!"

Max just standing there, taking another swig of his drink,
while watching the fight unfold, as the larger guy wearing a
grubby white vest, fading tattoos all over his arms to
knuckles, as the woman in question emerges from the flat,
with blood trickling from her nostrils also her right eye is
puffy. While another punch connects onto the side of the

skinnier guys eye sockets, but he doesn't crumble to floor again like the wall, instead comes up with an uppercut, his fist connecting beautifully on his unexpected chins, knocking him clean out, his lump of a body thudding the ground, nearly knocking down this god forsaken excuse of an apartment complex, which would be an improvement, as I said before this is a real shit hole of a place, not even vermin want to live here. While the skinny guy gets on one knee, as he is wiping the blood away from his nostrils also split lip. Max steps over the lump on the floor to carry on walking to his flat door at the end of the corridor.

Opening the door to his studio flat, as the woman over Max's shoulder is helping the skinner guy up, both walking back into her flat, for her to tend to his every need. Max slams the door behind him. Just being sacked from the only thing that mattered to him which was his science job, working in a lab with this worlds renowned established scientist.

His sofa bed still laying out, tattered bed covers lay scruffily on top. He hasn't got a lady to call his own or much money, he sits on his sofa bed looking around his flat which is falling apart, also dirty plates pilled up in the sink, along with takeaway containers from the Chinese down the road scattered around his apartment, a pile of dirty clothes beside a washing machine, with its door hanging on only by one screw in the hinge. Dark also dingy, the blinds broken in front of the only light source because there is no light bulb. Imagine a disgusting place to live then you will have the image I am portraying. Max letting out a sigh, taking a swig of whiskey, he pulls out a box of headache pills, paracetamol from his tattered coat pocket. Tearing open the box, he pushes all the pills out into his hand. He puts them into his mouth, chomping down while swigging at his whiskey. Finishing both the box also whiskey. He lays back on his brown sofa bed, which was originally grey, waiting for them to take effect, looking up at the paint chipped ceiling, his head swirling like a ceiling fan, lucky for him there isn't one in this place because it wouldn't work anyway.

He gets up, out of his bed, some time later. A light scattering tapping noise coming from his flats window, from the droplets of rain outside. Stumbling forwards toward the raggedy blinds to open the window for some fresh air, but darkness engulfs him as he collapses to the filthy carpet while dragging his hand across the dust-filled blinds, dust flickering up, off from them going airborne, lucky he didn't smash his head off the rusty radiator.

He stands in complete darkness.
Max shouts out, asking in a panicky voice "Hello! Hello! Anyone there!? I need help!"
A figure wearing a dark mystical robe with the earth, in all its glory rotating on his robes front, as the figure seems to be floating, approaching him, he is holding a black handled scythe.
A voice from the mysterious figure bellows out "Put your hands out!"
Max is trying to see a face from within the cloaks hood that belongs to the entity, all he sees is a reflection of himself, darkness with stars sparkling within between his head to the robes hood. Nervously Max places his hands out, palms up.
Without the mysterious reflections lips moving he says "I personally don't think you deserve this, but they do."
With the tip of the scythe he rips diagonally across both of Max's palms, but instead of crying out in pain the slits were painless. A glowing blue liquid seeps into the cuts, with that the mysterious figure walks away while muttering words, that belong to a different language under his breathe, sounds like the oldest language Tamil.

Max awakens on the dirty damp carpet of his flat because of a leak that's dripping from the decrepit ceiling, as a droplet falls splashing on the soaked carpet before his eyes, soaking in more, banging on his front door.

He mumbles "One minute."

But the person on the other side must not of heard him because the banging carries on, more furiously. Max gets up from the dirt damp carpet, he feels more awoken in himself, the bottle of whiskey smashed beside his bed, glass scattered some under the sofa bed. He goes to the door, crushing glass under his steps to see who is on the other side....

His landlord stands with a furious expression on his face with a strict demeanor. An older guy with bolding grey hair. Some stubble around his chin, tired eyes, over his shoulder you can see the tattooed geezer banging on his flat door, most probably while the younger guy is banging his misses.

The landlord says demandingly "Your rent is over due, Max."

Max responds with desperation in his voice "Hi Mr Digs, I was going to see you, funny story really, I lost my job today."

Mr Digs angrily says "Listen, that is not the only thing you will lose today, you have one hour to get your stuff out from the flat, you have run out of final warnings."

Max looks around the shit hole of his flat, thinking 'Even a pig would turn its nose up at this place.'

Mr Digs taps his gold Rolex watch, you know how he got that by over pricing people for shitty flats, as he is saying "Clocks ticking."

The raining tapping on his flats window suddenly stops, his landlord turns around, walking down the corridor, most probably to collect more rent money. Max puts his two fingers up, swearing at Mr Digs while mumbling "Fuck you."

A ray of ice alongside a stream of fire shoots out from Max's right hand. The fire hitting the back of his landlord, while the ice flies over the top of the steaming ash pile, hitting the once painted white chipped wooden banister, freezing around the wood. Max looks shocked along with confused in to what has just happened, how was it possible?

Max asks himself "where the fuck did that come from?"

He looks at his right hand that has the diagonal scar that is glinting with dark blue. After he checks his left hand, it is with a diagonal scar that has a light blue glint, swirling around the once open wound. He walks over to the ash pile to see, imbedded on top, a full set of nicotine stained teeth, Mr Digs Rolex, that's stopped working because, well he is dead, in a pile of ashes, along with his black wallet. Max grabs the wallet also of course the watch, wouldn't leave that there for someone else's sticky fingers, taking the clump of twenty also fifty pound notes out.

Max thinks to himself 'Today must have been rent day, now it's my fucking day.'

He drops the wallet on to the creaky floorboards while stashing the many Sterling pound notes in his pocket. I know you shouldn't wear a dead mans watch, but I don't blame Max for putting it on, I fucking would also I know you would, you know why it's a fucking real solid gold Rolex mate.

A cough from behind Max, which gets his attention, it is the tattooed big guy, fist still clenched because he was banging on the door, of his flat for his cheating old lady to let him in, but she is most probably riding the younger fitter geezer. He looks as confused as Max but instead of running for the hills, at the fact fire alongside ice just physically came out from the back of Max's hand, instead he comes thumping towards Max because he just see the clump of legal Sterling tender, that Max just stuffed into his pocket. So Max extends his right hands middle finger just to see if something happens, after a few seconds of pointing it towards the big fella. Max folds his middle finger down as a river of ice, streams out from the back of his hand, ice scattering around the big fella. Freezing him to the spot with fists still clenched, ready to throw a punch, because of the steaming ash pile causing the rooms temperature to rise suddenly also being so close to the frozen human statue, a drip thaws from his knuckles, running down to drip, the staircase on the other hand, has defrosted a bit more, a small puddle leaking through floorboards, Max noticing that, he decided before the big man thaws completely its best to make a move, as he carries on walk towards the stairs, he puts the Rolex on his left hand, not needing anything from his flat, not even looking back.

He finds a way outside the apartment at an latter stage, walking to the edge of the pavement, looking around one of this country's capital city's streets, still wet from the rain. The buildings opposite start collapsing, fire explodes out from top middle window above, shards of glass fall down, like an downpour of rain but you don't want to be kissing a lady under this downpour, it would ruin your romantic moment. Cars are on fire, some have been tipped upside down, with people still inside, maybe that is a lucky escape for them because some of the burnt corpses, laying on the pathway still clutching their singed shopping inside their fucking five pence bags, doesn't look the best way to go out. Max sees down the street a person running on fire, clutching a flaming briefcase. Max looks down to at his left hand wondering what shoots out from the back as he turns his....

A woman's voice screams "Watch out!"
Max looks around, eyes scanning around the carnage to see a woman in hiding, pointing above him, Max quickly looking up to see some of his flats buildings brickwork along with window falling towards him, he quickly runs forward in a state of panic, sliding over a silver car bonnet, ducking behind. The falling materials crashing to join the carnage below, like dropping a stone into a puddle, as pieces of bricks along with shards of glass clatter into the side of the car. Max sees the mature woman hiding behind a black public rubbish bin,

clutching the hand of her young son. He stands up looking back at his apartment complex to see an improvement, only joking, dust cloud impairing his vision from the fallen brickwork surrounds them like mist, slowly starting to settle.

The woman with her son comes out from behind the bin, coughing, waving the dust cloud don't know if it's helping, as they are walking towards Max, that is asking "What the F... is going on?"
The young boy points towards a pointy scaled dragon, swallowed by the dust cloud, but you still know it's there because it's a dragon hardly inconspicuous, as the creatures tail smashes into a crashed flame engulfed taxi, slow time, seeing in through the whispering flames flickering out from within the blown out window, to the taxi driver getting crispier as every millisecond passes, he tried to brush the flames off himself, but the temperature too much to brush away, back to normal time. While the engulfed taxi smashing through the office building, the crumbling brickwork that is falling to squash the woman, along with a black leather office chair also a desk is falling.
Max shouts "Quicker!"
He puts his left hand up, his fingers spread out, a light blue ray shoots out like a laser towards the building along with office equipment. Again slow time to see the full effects of the taxi tearing out of the office, following the path back to the road, the flames that was bursting out, slowly disappearing, extinguishing. Max can see the Indian taxi driver is inside, unharmed, while the office building is being repaired to its former glory, the stuff from within smashed on the concrete pavement, fixing itself as it travels back upwards, scorched bricks returning to orange, realigning with the crumbled cement, that's reattaching itself within, drying from wet to hard within the brickwork, as the taxis bonnet returning back to working, the taxi driver praising his blessings to still be alive, but if he isn't quick to save himself

this time, he might die again, so decides to jump out of his taxi, running across the road down an alley between two building.

Max shouts asking "Ha, oh fuck off! Did you see that? I just repaired that building, along with saved the taxi driver, sorry for swearing little man but come on that's amazing."

He continues to grab the hand, that belongs to the lady, all three start running away from the red fire breathing dragon. Darting between the cars trying to find a place to hide, a crushed bus flies over the top of them, a severed crushed hand falls out, nearly hitting the young boy. Thanks but I don't need a hand. The bus tumbles across the concrete road, crushing as well as taking everything with it until it smashes through the front of a local bakery. They can hear car alarms getting crushed from behind them some with bones breaking from once alive people, under the dragons weight. Feeling the heat from the flames that are being projected out of the dragons inner workings. They dart through an alley way, that is separating two buildings, black bin bags either side of the alleyway. They runs past a broken washing machine, a car is spinning through the air past the alleys entrance. They turn right out of the alley....

On to a housing estate, Max stops running knowing the dragon can't get through the alley, along with step over buildings. The lady rushing ahead practically dragging her son along the road, like having to go to see your aunt when you was a kid, but you didn't want too, much rather of played footie with your mates.

The lady calling back "Thank you, I am Zarah, this is my son Earnie."

Max is practically jogging to keep up with her, while introducing himself, she sharply turns into a garden path, leading up to a house with a red door. Max follows closely behind.

He asks "Hold on, what's the rush?"

Zarah responds saying "My son needs his diabetes medication."

Zarah taking her keys from her coat pocket, fiddling around trying to get the key into the doors lock, panicking, snapping it in the process, she quickly gets frustrated. As she is just about to swear but contains herself.

"Mummy, I don't feel well." Comes from the young boy, getting more paler as each second passes. Before Zarah can respond, A light blue ray is pulling the broken key tip, out from the doors keyhole, floating through the air, fixing back onto the other key part, that Zarah is pinching.

Max says "Try again, if it happens again, I will kick your door in because little one is looking ill, also I could do with a cuppa, along with drain the lizard before I face this."

Zarah says "Thanks."

She tries it for the second time, more calmly, her homes front door opens.

Max sitting down on a black leather couch inside Zarah's home, Earnie watching a kids program on the television. Zarah comes into the living room from her beautiful dining room, in the background, with two cups, she hands one to Max.

While saying "I hope you like it."

Max responds saying "That's champion, thanks."

Not wasting no time, he takes a sip after puts it on a glass coaster, sitting on top of her coffee table. While Zarah sits beside him, hooking a lock of her dark black hair behind her ear.

Max asks "Where is your husband? I see the pictures along with the wedding ring, on your finger, you know don't mean to be rude."

Zarah responds saying "Unfortunately, he is no longer with us."

Max says "Oh, I am sorry to hear that."

Zarah says "Don't be, it happened when Earnie was a year old, I have spent my time grieving over the loss of a good man, but he knew it was coming, left us comfortable."

Max nods while leaning over to grab his cup of char.

Zarah asks "Anyway, what the hell is going on out there? I mean dragons, they're a mythical creatures, make-believe by other imaginary minds."

Max responds saying "I know, I didn't think he would be able to do, but it explains a few things."

Zarah responds asking "Like what?"

The cartoon characters on the t.v screen, screaming in terror while the village is getting decimated by a dragon, spewing fire.

Max says "Let me cast your mind into this."

Like a droplet of water onto my cinema canvas, the images ripple out to a time, where Max while explaining word for word to Zarah, how he believes this has come to be. "I was walking down a corridor, towards one of the labs that I used to work in, an assistant to Mr Bernard Bunsen."

Zarah cuts in saying "Oh I have herd of him, a top scientist in his field."

Max carries on saying "Yes he is, my first day I was like a cat that got the cream, when I found out I was going to be his assistant, but I had been working with him for like a year by this time, I was walking down the corridor, glancing right into other lab rooms on my way, seeing people wearing lab coats, working. By this time I have arrived at my lab, walking into the room, Bernard is looking through the ocular lens on his microscope, so I said "Hello."

But a grunt like usual he is always engrossed in his work. I went to go get changed, but he stopped his work walking over to me with his crazy white hair. There was something different with his eyes, like he hadn't slept for a few days, but something wild was gleaming through the tiredness. He offers his hand for me to shake saying "So I am sorry to tell you, but I will no longer be needing your services. I have completed my project, thank you for your services."

I shake his hand, then grab my stuff, leaving with my dignity still in tact, I could of smashed up the whole place, but no point, would have been in bracelets in the back of a paddy wagon, because of my temper, nah fuck that. But what I do know he was working on a secret project, in a secret lab, I know he has played a part in these mythical creatures returning.

The colorful droplet reemerging out from my cinema canvas, the imaging changes back to Max, Zarah engrossed into what he was telling her. Her son still engrossed into cartoons on the television, looking better after his diabetic medicine, most probably didn't hear a word that Max said, but Zarah did.

Zarah asks "So how can you do all the stuff with your hands? Did he experiment on you?"

Max explains to her how he got gifted hands while sipping on his drink.

Chaos running through the street, outside of her living room window, you can see people running in terror, Max stands up.

He says "Thank you for the cuppa, best use these gifted hands to stop this prick, before he turns civilization to destruction."

Zarah gives Max a hug while saying "Send the people you save to me, I will keep them safe."

He goes "You're too kind, stay safe, c'ya youngster."

Earnie still watching the cartoons on the television. After he walks to the front door to open it up, entering into the chaos that is running rampant on the streets.

Max while standing on the door step of Zarah's home, the door shuts behind him, a few seconds of watching the chaos unfold down the road, trying to find what is causing the horrified mood to spread, he sees the same dragon, destroying everything, man has built quicker than it took them to build, as the mythical creature stomps up the road, crushing cars like they're juice cartons being stepped on, remember doing that as a kid, trying to get the straw to fire out, when it does goes miles, being the coolest thing ever as a kid. Out of thin air seven Primates appear, they don't have to look around for long to see something to rip apart, the dragon trying to fend off the group of Primates, go read my book, *An Essence Of Time.* to see how they look, with their eyes. A Primates tail latches on to a scale that belongs to the dragon, ripping it away from the creatures flesh, that is scorching another flame filled Primate, that's running around making all kinds of noises while becoming crispier, the canal of flames stop coming out from the dragons insides as it's raining down burning everything on its path, flickering off from the roads tarmac, like a chef torching a Crème brûlée, to make it more caramelized. As two Primates start to climb the dragon like rock climbers, just without all the harnesses. Like peeling a scab off as the other Primate flings the scale away, smashing through a betting shops window, as it goes to take another shiny red scale off from the dragon, like a daring shoplifting returning to the scene of his crime to do it all over again, but doesn't get away because from above is the dragons large foot descending, you know what they say about large feet, big socks. Squashing down on the Primate, breaking every bone in its frame, like when you get a coke can, drinking it all to stamp on it. This would be the perfect time to be a looter, to get yourself all kinds of things because the old bill are trying to kill the other creatures so they are struggling to keep order, so who is going to stop you from running in to all the shops, taking the cash out of the registers, but you have to know the cities streets well, to survive from being killed by the different creatures roaming around causing terror. Max starts walking down the street, as people are frantically running past, people in cars honking their horns trying their hardest to get away from being the creatures next victim, Max doesn't get too far up the road before within a blue flash of light he is gone.

We are strolling down a corridor to the bottom where a closed lonely door stands, a big window on the left overlooking the city, some parts of the building, that once stood strong, with clouds whispering past their tops, but now lay in ruins. Fire desperately engulfing the parts it can, a piece of paper, burning up as it is caught in the wind, floating through the air until it is stopped by the window, it appears to be a contract, ashes floating away from the burning pages. Reaching the bottom of the corridor, walking through the door to see what is inside.

Mr Bunsen stands frantically pressing buttons on a control panel, inside of his secret lab, but nothing's working to stop the time machine in the corner from, shooting rays of black with a red tinge, smashing out a side window, to a roof of a parking lot, bringing something else back from the past, as it starts forming, bones collecting inches above from concrete roof, it really starts, coming to life, muscles start forming around the creatures skeleton... .

Max appearing inside a time within the worlds history, the part of An Essence Of Time. The first thing his eyes lock onto is a mammoth, as it perambulating not far in the distance, feeling its steps from where he is standing, not wanting to be killed in unfamiliar surroundings, he goes to raise his fist, just about to release a finger on his right hand for fire or ice to shoot out from the back of. But is stopped by a giant, the original owners of this earth.
With a voice so deep, enough to shake any human to its very core.

"Don't do it, our elders know of the power that your hands hold, we need your help in return, Sterling will help you."

The roaring of the king Primate seems to be getting closer, the massive creatures roar shaking branches on trees, now you might think well that could be wind, well you should feel the beating sun on your face without feeling any type of breeze on your skin, this can't be my city.

Max looks up in shock, being the biggest human, that someone from the 21st century has ever locked eyes on, apart from on a cinema screen.

Max responds asking "Where did you come from?"

The giants response is saying "I am one of the original owner of earth, when dinosaurs roamed with us, anyway come, no time wasting."

Max responds saying "I don't think I have much of a choice, okay, it seems like time is of the essence, so let's go."

The giant grunts leaning on his battle axes handle while kneeling down, like an elderly gentleman using his walking stick to pick something up from the ground, but for the giant it's for Max to get on him.

Max taking a second to look at the facial features, that belong to the original earths protector, long strands of darkened grey hair coming from his chin, goatee separated down the middle by a lush green vine on each side, every strand neatly packed.

Max asks "What are you brushing your beard with?"

The giant responds saying "Hedgehog."

Max makes a face of 'Fair enough' after asks "What are you doing?"

The giant responds "Get on, I take you, we get there quicker, with your earthling steps, we won't get there for another week."

Max responds saying "Just so you know, I don't agree with riding you but earth hasn't got a week, well I know my version hasn't."

Max is climbing up the leg of the giant, his leg hairs are like like vines in a jungle, Max feels like Tarzan raised him.

The giant says "This is earth, you have gone back in time to be shown how the first types of civilization begun. The chaos roaming through your version of time in earth hasn't started yet, but will be worse if what you do here is not dealt with, so it will help you later."

Max still scaling up the Giant which starts to stand up, Max going from Tarzan to a mountain climber, he starts using the chunks in the giants flesh to his advantage, most probably from past battles, won or lost but the remaining scars left behind on the giants body, as memories, his right hand latches into the scar, he goes to lift his foot into another, on the top of the giants arm, Max's left hands fingers clutching beside his right hands fingers....

Max see's the giant as a child peering through a bush at something which hasn't become apparent to us but I am sure it will, he is about the same size as Max, but more broader, which is watching on from beside us. A forest floor quickly forms under our feet, the clearing he is looking out of is a caves entrance, beside a stream, clear water passing through, different types of stream fishes swimming. Now he was told beforehand not to come anywhere near here, by his elders, because this cave belongs to as Max has already met one of these, the cloaked person from earlier that gave Max his powers. Not sure if it is the same one. Max walking up to the side of the kid giant, but he doesn't acknowledge him, still peering out. The both of them not acknowledging us, as the figure has ahold of a Sky Glider, his floating hand is grasping ahold of the Sky Gliders bloody, beating brain, that's ripped out from the creatures skull, blood dripping down the creatures forehead dripping off from the top of the creatures eye sockets, the fire within his eyes glow, growing. The world still rotating on the figures cloak, as a ray of Samarium metal shavings, shoots out from the tip of his scythe, witch is made from Wolframite, the same material makes the SMW mask. The giant elders call these the SMW. The shards of Samarium oxidizing as it starts moving across the waist of the Sky Glider, tearing through like a welder cutting a shape out of metal, sparks flying like a lit sparkler, intestine spilling out. SMW controlling the creature to walk towards the stream, before they get into the stream, the shards stop coming out. The Sky creatures tail splashing as it's dragged deeper into the water, Stoney bottom, dunking the Sky Glider, water absorbing to shooting through the other creatures wings, defense mechanism working still. Water splashing up the creatures mid-section. SMW pulling him up from his dunk, walking him out, to the side of the giant, a twig snaps but can't see who it is. The crystal clear water now murky from the Sky Gliders blood, chunks of intestines floating but are soon gobbled up by the fishes. Leaving a trail a watered down blood up the streams bank to the caves entrance, where the shards of Samarium resume out from his scythe, oxidation happens in its route back to the Sky Gliders mid-section, purple smoke on impact. The giant shooing away a buzzing bee. This alerts the SMW to the child giant, that get a ray of Samarium towards him, the child king of Primates, glides through the air, through Max pushing the kid giant out of harms way, the oxidized shards still scorch through the kid giants skin, blood surfacing. The child king Primate saved to help escape with the kid giant, saving themselves from any more danger....

The scar that Max's hands are clutching onto starts healing, as he quickly rushes up onto the giants shoulder, walking to the middle, trying not to loose his balance, he sits down.

The giant says "Watch out for Sky Gliders, fire creatures with wings as sharp like my battle axe, they are all black, like flies around shit.

Max responds saying "Okay, I will keep an eye out, we must be the shit then."

The giant starts walking as Max perches himself on his right shoulder.

While they walk away, Max touches the giants cheek, smooth as you like, while asking "So what do you use to shave the rest of your face?"

The giant whistles loudly to get the mammoths attention, while answering Max's question "Sky gliders wings or Armadillos shell, depend what I see first.

Max responds asking "Nice, which one do you prefer?"

The giant responds saying "Wings, shell is harder to hold also need to be sharpened, but you do get a two in one, because you can boil armadillo to eat for breakfast to have a shave after."

Max asks "Oh, Sky gliders aren't nice to eat?"

The giant responds with a shake of his head, side to side, as the mammoth is nearly at their side.

Birms, Manc, Cambs, Lon alongside Liver are walking around the corner of a massive boulder. Also in my original book An Essence Of Time, go read it to see whom they are. Sunshine glistening off from the rocks surface, Cambs stops his brothers in their tracks, putting his arm out, because he has spotted in the distance, a mammoth being attacked by a Sea Dweller, that has sent a projectile vomit of ice, towards, freezing the mammoths front right leg. While a Sky Glider like a fly hovering around shit, is sending spit fires down, but not at the Sea Dweller or the Mammoth, but towards the giant with Max standing on the original ancient guardians shoulder. They are dodging the spit fires coming towards them until Max sends back an element of his own, ice souring through the air like an majestic golden eagle, until crashing around the Sky Glider, like tree roots growing underground making its way around the Sky Gliders body, now gravity has begun to do its job, because the Sky Glider can't flap its wings, so its falling to the ground, rapidly, like it couldn't of been more perfect because the frozen Sky Glider is absorbed by a scale that belongs to the Sea Dweller, within a matter of milliseconds the frozen Sky Glider is catapulted out. Max not wanting to waste anytime he sends flames down towards the Sea Dweller, that is still attacking the Mammoth, that's getting far or even learning too much, because every time it freezes the bottom legs of the Mammoth, the massive land creature just stamps, which cracks the ice off, seeing in the distance, the frozen Sky Glider thuds into a rock, the ice could of broken off on impact but it most probably broke its back or neck. The Mammoth is stamping at the Sea Dweller, along with lashing its trunk at the backing up Sea Dweller. Max trying to get the aim correct because each ball of flames he sends down to the Sea Dweller, either gets absorbed to then make him shit himself because he now knows they can fire back out from anywhere, or they miss exploding beside. The Sea Dwellers razor sharp tail slashes through the hair of the Mammoth, like rain fall brown hairs trickledown. But the Sea Dwellers persistence in whipping its sharp tail at the Mammoths legs eventually draws blood from a gash, that's leaking out mixing with the woolly mammoths fur, feeling the pain from the gash the large creature goes wild, stamping at will while ramming with its tusks, unlucky for the Sea Dweller its defense mechanism hasn't come in handy this time, because the tusk went through the creatures scale, out of another scale as the Mammoth lifting the Sea Dweller off the ground, lashing it's tail but not getting far, out of range. Four Primates traveling through the land, spot the Woolly Mammoth with the Sea Dweller stuck on its tusk, they decide to go to attack the Mammoth, because why wouldn't you.

A Primate sends a bone dart which shuts down the Sea Dweller on impact, right between its eyes. Max freezes one after sets another Primate on fire, leaving two left but that soon becomes one, because the Primates frame can't take the weight of the Mammoth, stamping all over him, with the Sterling settlement protectors still watching from the sidelines, we are standing beside them. The last Primate sending bone darts while darting around his frozen comrade, past the flaming Primate, that's running around trying to put the fire that's spreading, scorching his skin out, until it collapses to the ground, twitching. The Primate then skips around the squashed one, like a footballer avoiding a tackle, sending bone darts out like a arrows from a huntsman, but the bone darts are quickly frozen by Max, they fall to the ground below. The Primates run is cut short to get to Max because of the Mammoths other tusk, splitting the monkey in two, as the ivory tusk is soon turnt bloody. As the creatures body is pushed further up the tusk leaving pieces of flesh all over, blood dripping off from the tusk, that pushes more of the creatures guts to the mud below, as it slaps onto the ground. The giant slides the creatures off from the blood covered ivory tusk, tossing them to the side, for the other animals to feast on. While Max is climbing down, when Max makes it back down onto terra-firma, walking over to the Mammoths leg, were the skin is open, blood absorbing into the surrounding woolly coat, the Mammoth looking not knowing if he should trust the earthling, Max with his healing hand, trying to reattach the creatures skin, the giant is stroking the Mammoths back like a person petting mans best friend, a light blue ray of energy shoots out of Max's hand to wrap around, the skin appearing to heal until there is no longer blood seeping.

The Giant says loudly "Let's get going!"

Max looks up while he nods, while the lights blue energy around the Mammoths leg, starts to disappear into thin air, the Giant bends down, with his massive hand flat, Max climbs on to the hand as the Giant raises his hand, like an elevator taking him higher, passing levels until it's one he needs to get off at, Max in the middle of his palm, the giant stops his hand at the side of the Mammoths back.

Max asks "He isn't going to kick off is he, if I get on his back?"

The giant responds saying, loudly "No, he recognized you as a friend, because you heal his leg, otherwise you would look like squashed Primate!"

Max makes his way onto the back of the Mammoth, making his way to the head through its fur, like a adventurous person making their way through dense forest, Max is trying to get comfortable.

Max says "You know you need to chill with your voice, I have ears mate."

A cheeky smile forms on the giants sandpaper face. All three carry on with their journey, with the Sterling settlement protectors in hot pursuit.

The giant, with Max riding on the Mammoths back, appear out from a clearing of a forest, to a beautiful lake with mist rising off from the lapping waters, while a vulture is eating the drying flesh off from the mammoths tusk, the giant shoo's the vulture away *wings flapping, getting quieter.* as he takes the mammoth to the edge of the lake to clean them. The giant just about to say something, but is stopped by commotion happening behind them, causing both to look behind, even the mammoth looks. Maxes eyes adjusted to see where the noise is coming from, seeing through the tree branches, somethings, in the woods are fighting amongst themselves.

Max says "Get me down I want to see what is going on."

While Max makes his way to see what is going on, let's go see for ourselves what's happening my friend. We make our way through the branches, swiftly, avoiding bumping into anything.

Manc is pointing his earth sword at an oncoming Primate, the rocks that lay dormant on the muddy ground start to wiggle, some pushing their way from beneath, buried under twigs, to smash into the Primate, until it's stoned to death like how some people were killed back, a long time ago, not stoned in a high way, you would definitely prefer the second kind of stoned, you know what I'm saying. Anyway, another Primate hanging from a branch, shooting bone darts towards the Sterling settlement protectors, Lon just about to get the primitive creatures when he hears...

"Nah bro, this one is mine."

Cambs interject, as Birms ducks out of the way of a bone dart which sticks into the bark of a tree behind, Birms nearly getting hit by the closed tail of another Primate, which he starts fighting, in front is Cambs that shocks the hanging Primate, literally as a lightning bolt is dispersed from his sword, shocking through the the creatures body to its wrapped around tail, causing his tail to unravel, falling to the earth below like how Lucifer was supposed to of, a flaming arrow is flying through the air like a homing missile, locked onto its target, as the ignited arrow explodes into the falling Primate.

Cambs asks surprisingly "Fuck was that?!"

Cambs looks around to see Archie, with his new flaming bow, still extended, he is wearing the same armory as Cambs, that was crafted by the old man in the forest, but there is a few more things, that Archie can do but you will see that later mate. Lon is taking on another Primate, *Ding.* as a bone dart is ricocheting off his sword, that is diagonally covering his face, so Lon changing stance to pointing as he smacks the butt of his water sword, the Primate instantly starts to shrivel up like to when you stay in the bath too long, to a raisin. As the creature falls to the mud below, water starts to seep from the wrinkled Primate, that water soon turns to blood, which is running through the cracked mud, mixing with different dirty leaves along with twigs, that have fallen from the trees above. Birms gets his sword taken by the last Primates tail, that wraps around the sharp blade, cutting its tail in the process, as it flings the mysterious weapon to one side, that clambers along the forest ground, the other settlement protectors go to rescue their brother, from the angry Primate, showing its razor sharp teeth at Birms, that steps back only to feel a tree stop him, he can't be stepping back anymore, the Primates tail ball, starts to open in quarters, ready to release bone bone darts or latch on to a limb, with claws at the ready to rip through human flesh, so Birms shrugs, as he puts his fists up ready to fight, just before the settlement protectors save Birms, an icicle dart enters into the side of the Primates head, slow motion. Some blood spurts outwards, splattering up the icicle. Instantly killing the primitive creatures, as its body, lifeless, thumps the dirty ground. The settlement protectors stopped in their tracks, to see Max with his hand extended, his fingers making the peace sign towards them, to whoever or whatever that want to bring harm behind it's a fuck you.

After they have all introduced themselves, Max takes them to see the Giant that is resting on a giant rock beside the lake, while the Mammoth is grazing on the surrounding vegetation, droplets of blood tinted water dripping off the giants hands resting on the bottom of his battle axe, because he has cleaned the mammoths once bloodied tusks. The settlement protectors notice the giant straight away, as he is the one that helped them defeat the Sky Gliders Queen.

The giant says "We have to go, it won't be easy to defeat the Primates king."

Cambs responds saying "Before we head off, can I say a thanks to you for helping us back there also making sure we didn't have to give Birms an early funeral, also to the giant a thanks for helping us defeat the Queen."

As the others second what Cambs said, the giant places his fist to his chest where his heart is, beating, after bows his head. They all get ready to go, with Archie now joining the settlement protectors to go with Max along with the giant to see what their journey awaits.

while they're traveling through the earths land on their pursuit to kill the Primitive king, the other men that come down to the earth are in the ship, that belong to Estuary also his brother, which are at the helm with the other leaders standing around them, as Estuary is turning the hand carved ancient ships wheel, so much detail in one object from every battle, Estuary, his brother also their crew have faced, have been carved into the ships wheel after their victories. The crew onboard doing their jobs at maintaining the ship to stay healthy. Oceans salt water crashing into the side of the ships changing sides, that has changed to a battle, that all the ships crew participated in, with a sea creature that become extinct afterwards, on their planet. The ships side is of Estuary slaying the sea beast by decapitation, as the creatures long, enormous eel type body smashes over the ships deck, nearly snapping the ship in half, as the sea beasts head, is pushed off by their men, rolling off before it breaks through the decking, splashing into the lapping waves below followed by the creatures blood mixed with guts spewing out. They lost a lot of good men that day also in past battles, to this sea creature along with other ships, that used to sail the waters on his planet, that now lay at the bottom on the seas murky bottom, skeletons that have had their skin along with organs picked, to feed the fishes, along with the ship wrecks that became the fishes homes, also shelter from the many other bigger sea creatures, that roam their ocean, on their world there is a little bit less land, so they sail the oceans a lot that's why their ships are battle hardened. Their planet is beside our moon, you see it more at night as a star, faded during the evening leading up to the night.

Back to the present day, to Mr Bunsen, that is in his lab trying to get his handmade time machine, which is a dark metallic globe on a stand, with the outlines of the country's glowing gold, the outline of a clocks face glowing gold, with numbers, one to twelve situated around along with hands glowing the same, clocks hands berserkly spinning around, that are situated in one of the globes many oceans. Mr Bunsen trying his hardest to stop his time machine from working by itself, sending mythical creatures forward to this time in earths history, where they will cause more damage than good. A guy in a white lab coat bursts through the door, disturbing Mr Bunsen as he is trying to save humanity, ironically without meaning to, he is the one that started this destruction.

Anyway, the man says "Bernard, we have to go, before we get overrun by these fucking things, there is a chopper on the roof."

Before Mr Bunsen can say anything, one of the mans brown eyes are forced out from its socket, followed by the other one, oh shit imagine that slowed down, seeing the bone penetrating through the back of the mans skull, X-ray to see the bone darts traveling through his brain, killing all that knowledge, such a waste, for them to push his eyes through his eyes lid, as he was blinking. Now I hear you ask, why don't he destroy the time machine? Well my friend you find the answer to your question later, I am sure of that. As the lab coat guys body slumps onto the tiled flooring, twitching, the eyes roll across the floor until Bernard, stops them with the tip of his shoe, looking down at them, the eyes crossed like a person with that eye condition. Hearing the snarling from the crazed Primate, that is running from the end of the corridor, so Mr Bernard Bunsen runs forward, squashing an eye in the process, nearly slipping as he has to pull the lab coat guy into the room after he slams the door shut oblivious to how far the Primate is, rushing to lock it with panic proving to be difficult, but he manages to. As he starts stepping back from the door, two bone darts brake through the doors wood, shards of wood brake away falling to the ground, bone darts get stuck in the process, Mr Bunsen searching for weapons to defend himself around the lab.

A blue flash happens in front of Bernards eyes, also your mans well the one that isn't squished, while the Primate is still crashing into the door, but the lock withstanding the pounding, Max appears from the blue flash, to most likely save Bernard from his fatal death, another bone dart cracks apart way through the door followed by the Primate smashing against the door, the lock partly bursts from the door, a screw holding it on. Mr Bunsen looking shocked at the fact Max just appeared from thin air. While Max puts his hand out, a ray of blue light, extends from his palm to the lock, that is just about hanging on, fixing it, as the screws start to travel back from the floor, up the door back into the lock, screwing themselves in, just in time because the Primate thuds into the door again but this time, it doesn't burst open.

Max says asking "Hello Mr Bunsen, surprised to see me? You should start fixing the time machine, instead of looking gobsmacked, no time to waste you know."

Mr Bunsen still a little startled, puts down a screwdriver that he was using to build the time machine, but this time around it would of been to defend himself from the Primate, as he goes back to the control panel to fix it.

Mr Bernard Bunsen responds asking "What is going on? Where did you come from?"

Before Max can respond, the Primate smashing into the door again, but not gaining access, another bone dart bursts in the door, lodging into the wood, like a squatter finding a way into a cabin in a forest. Max moves his hand to heal the parts of the door that have been done dart infested.

While Max explains what happened to him since being sacked by Mr Bunsen, shards of wood on the floor start sliding backwards, towards the door. A light shoots out from the time machine, to a building outside, a pterodactyl starts to form on top of the roof, bones jointing together.....

As the pterodactyl is squawking on top of the building, takes flight off the roof to cause carnage. The army on the streets, trying to contain the destruction, also trying to keep as many people as possible alive. Mr Bunsen is trying to fix the root of the problem, while Max is keeping the door from being knocked down by the raging Primate. Another bone dart breaks through the door, shards burst from its impact, Max is quick to heal it, while walking towards the door, his palm out. Mr Bunsen working hard behind him, as the shards burst backwards, the bone dart squeezing back out, before the shards can repair back into the door, Max closes his heeling hand, with his right eye, he looks through the hole that the last bone dart left out from, seeing through the Primate jaws snapping, tail open ready to strike or send, sending another bone dart towards the peeping eye.

Max says "Fuck that!."

Max moving his head out of the way to let him have the ice from the other hand, through the hole, the ice travels through the air, engulfing the oncoming bone dart in mid air, as the rest freezes to the Primate, looking like a ice sculpture, a pissed off one at that.

Max says "That shut you up."

He heals the door before going up to Mr Bunsen, that is working.

Estuary's ship sailing through the oceans salt water, the sun rays gleaming off the freshly mopped floor. The crew taking a break from their jobs on their ship, but the only person that can't take a break is the captain, Estuary. He is at the ships helm, turning the wheel towards the land in the distant, Seagulls flying above.

Stoner says "This is a beautiful world, shame that the creatures on it, want to destroy everything."

Estuary responds saying "I second that brother, the ocean is relaxed here, on our world you don't know what your going to get."

Inferno asks "Is this ship strong enough to deal with all different weather elements?"

Estuary responds saying "Oh yeah brother, we upgrade it when needed, there is always work being done."

Inferno nods as he responds saying "Nice bro, I like the wheel, a lot of detail on one thing."

Inferno is looking at the ships wheel more closely as Estuaries hands are controlling the ship, they are wearing their respected elementary armor.

Estuary responds saying "Thanks bro, carved it myself after we win a major battle."

Stoner says "I am glad that we all bumped into the Sterling settlement protectors."

Inferno responds saying "Yeah they have taken us in like family."

Estuary asks Inferno "What's it like on your world?"

"I can imagine it's fucking boiling, you would need a bit of me up there to cool it down." Comes from the silent but observing Neon.

Inferno responds saying "Well to outsiders it would seem hot."

In the distance the faded moon is still out, with two smaller planets either side that belong to the element keepers, looking like a belt, I used to see on wrestling.

Inferno carries on saying "It's not bad just a lot of natural fire combustion you have to be careful of when traveling because they can come from underground, out of nowhere, but don't last too long.

A crew member walks up to Estuary, with food along with another crew member that is holding drinks, they offer them something to drink also a bite to eat, thank you very much.

Max is still alongside Mr Bunsen, that is near completion on shutting the time machine down but without destroying it. While Bernard is saying "There is a chopper on the roof."

Max is looking out one of the window walls within the lab. He is looking down at the destruction below, firemen trying to put the fires out caused by the dragon also other fire breathing creatures, police trying to be in control of all the situations, along with calming scared people down. The army are trying to get people out from the city, loading different cultured humans into lorries like cattle for the slaughter house, while the ambulance crew members are doing what they do best, trying to save lives along with healing the cuts or burns that some people have sustained.

The pterodactyl flies past, a Sky Glider being crushed between its enormous beak, tossing it towards the window that Max is standing behind. In slow motion, you can see the panic on Maxes face form, as he turns while running away from the window, shouting something at Mr Bunsen, while the Sky Glider rolling through mid-air, blood droplets from puncture wounds spiraling out from the Sky Gliders body, that crashes through the window. Shards of glass explode as the creature impacts through. The Sky Gliders body skims across the labs ground, like a stone skimming across the waters surface, until the creature crashes into the bottom of a cupboard. Back to normal speed as a test tube rocks on the counter until eventually falling off, smashing onto the Sky Gliders head.

Max standing alongside Mr Bunsen, with the Sky Gliding wreckage at their feet's.

Bernard says "A bit cold now, he decided to open the window for us."

Max responds saying "I know, very nice of him."

Max walks over to the window to put an end to the breeze, as Bernard goes over to the time machine, to make sure it shuts down smoothly.

Bernard says "It should be shut down in a few minutes, listen I am sorry for letting you go, but I didn't want anyone to get hurt."

As shards of glass are backtracking towards the empty hole within the window frame, fixing itself back together, like a puzzle.

Max responds saying "I know but not many things go to plan in life."

The Sky Glider is trying to make it back to his feet, blood dripping from puncture holes in its body, to a forming puddle below, as the Sky Glider is nearly standing up freezing water starts forming around the creatures body, even freezing a blood droplet as it drips. Max acknowledged the fact a fire would ruin the lab, because they might need it later.

Max steps out from doorway followed by Bernard, that is wheeling the global time machine, on an white trolley onto the rooftop, hearing the chopper, looking around seeing it with fellow scientists within the black chopper. As the chopper's blades making a lot of noise, not a good thing with a pterodactyl patrolling the sky. The other scientists calling for the both of them to hurry up, but their shouting muffled by the chopper.

Max says "Go! When it's time I will come back to sort this out with you!"

Bernard nods as he starts walking towards the chopper, with people inside, waving him towards them. Mr Bunsen stops to turn to say something to Max, but he has already disappeared.

The anchors have already been released, they are currently sinking to the oceans bed, as the ship floats sideways to a shoreline. The side of the ships towering body is displaying a battle between all three of this earths creatures. A triple threat you could say, as a Sky Glider is sending a Sea Dweller a spit fire, the Sea Dweller sending a lunging Primate, a projectile vomit of ice, the Primate sending bone darts towards a Sky Glider, that has begun taking flight. Four rope ladders fall from the ships top, as Estuary,

Stoner, Inferno along with Neon, start coming down the ladders, that are clattering into the ships side. Estuaries brother is staying at the ships helm to keep it guarded along with safe from the Sky Gliders.

Max reappears in the world of An Essence of Time, go buy it please! He opens his eyes to be looking down a swords blade, that is pointing at his throat. His eyes taking in the exquisite shape along with pattens, that makes up such a sword, now by this time I am sure you are wondering, along with itching to ask, who this blade belongs to? Well it belongs to one of the few dwarf guards, that keep anything evil from entering through, the brown hand carved double doors, to the dwarf kingdom, with bushes mixed with trees either side of the doors. Max about to fight raising his hand to let out his protection, but he is stopped by the giant, behind placing his gigantic index finger on, taking up the whole of Maxes right shoulder, each of the giants fingernails looking like a gigantic pizza, like the ones I used to make at the restaurant I worked at.

The giant says "Easy there earthling, we need these people."

Max puts his hand down at the same time as the dwarf, putting his sword back into its holster. Two dwarf guards stand side by side of the dwarf kingdoms entrance. Max looks around to see the Sterling settlement protectors beside the giant.

The dwarf guard asks "What is your business here?"

The giant shouts responds saying "We need to speak with your king! Can you take us to him?"

Max says "You know he can hear you, he is only a bit smaller than us."

The dwarf guard responds asking "How do I know your not here to start a war?"

The giant bellowing out a laugh, shaking trees in his laughs process, after responds saying "Because I wouldn't start a war like this, that's firstly, secondly, our kinds have never had a war, thirdly I am a earths protector, which means I took an oath to keep evil things from destroying the good also the earth, I can carry on like the fourth reason being I don't start wars for no reason, I only get involved in them if needed. So take us to your king because time is running out."

The dwarf guard looks more stumped than he already is, after lets them pass, the other guards open the wooden door. On the other side is just more overgrown forest, but when they step through the doorway, they swirl after zapped, disappearing to hopefully the dwarf kingdom.

Let's go check on what Estuary also the others are up to, as their boots are trudging through the wet soil, must of rained the night before here, each step moving the mud into small trenches, squelching.

Stoner asks "Do you know what they are?"

As he points towards something, following to where he is pointing to, there is several black pods that have grown out of the ground. Walking towards them they notice a green substance coursing through the black shell of the pods.

Inferno says asking "Is it safe to go to them? We don't know what they are or why they are there?"

Estuary responds saying "We can look but not touch, there is nothing around protesting us not to."

Neon says "That's true."

They carry on walking over to the pods, which are on the outskirts of a small forest that's at the foot of a rocky mountain.

Mate you need to see this, come on have a watch with me, we enter into the dwarf kingdom, along side the others. As they are walking through the city towards the kings castle, situated at the head of the kingdom. The small folks that call this place their home are gawping at the Giant, that is clearly out of place, even Max along with the Sterling settlement protectors are taller but not that much. The architecture within this place is exquisite, everything is hand carved stone, by the dwarf stone masons. There are dwarf kids sitting on stone benches, watching a play being performed by their elders, of a battle of theirs, many moons ago. A dwarf is dressed like a Sea Dweller in a leafy costume, that has a tail of the Sea Dweller tied on by a vine, walking through the wooden scenery, that has been made to look like trees, a dwarf warrior, in their black armor, that is sitting in a tree, undetected, with a bow, loaded with an arrow, letting the blunted arrow go, the on-fours dwarf Sea Dweller catches it near his armpit, standing up doing a spin after dropping down pretending to be dead in a dramatic way. The dwarf kids start clapping along with cheering also laughter.

Estuary is walking with the others through the forest, until they come to an ancient decrepit stone ruins. Unbeknown to them it belongs to a race of lizard, shapeshifter people. which start emerging from the crumbling stone entrances. The outsiders, Neon, Stoners, alongside Estuary take their swords out, ready to strike on any one of them. The lizard shapeshifters, walking over towards the four of them, with human features such as a head, torso with arms hands, midsection with legs feet attached. But their physical features are that of lizards to the eyes, no hair, skin which is scales, to their mouths, not a stitch of clothing on them. Hemipenes waving in the wind like you wouldn't believe. The dominant leader steps forward out of their small gathering of different species, the leader is Glizzie, he is apart of the Thorny Devil species.

Glizzie hissing while saying "I can smell the fear on you humans."

Estuary responds with laughter, as he says "I don't believe you can."

Estuary sniffs the air around the lizard leader.

After says "I can smell bullshit, it's coming out of your slits."

Glizzie asks "If you have done anything to our harvest, we will wage war on your kind, we will obliterate all of you."

Inferno is quick to pull his sword after hearing that, as the others get ready to kill, Estuary is quick to cool the situation by saying....

"We looked but didn't touch them, you know we are not made of glass, we won't smash easily."

There is a shadow that goes through them all on the ground, from something above, flying in the sky.

The situation is quickly escalated but not by either one of the groups, but by a pod, smashing between them. As a group of Sky Gliders have harvested the lizards people crops for them, isn't that nice? I don't think Glizzie is too pleased. Another pod smashes on the ground followed by few more, green liquid babies splashing all over the place, as baby lizard shapeshifters spill out from the pods, rolling across the ground snapping through their umbilical cord, The Primate kings roar shakes the ground even the three airborne Sky Gliders shake. Which makes Inferno's aim not to its best as a blazing ball, engulfed in flames misses its intended target, but the second one don't, fire combusts all over the falling Sky Glider. As the other one sends a spit fire down, that explodes over an empty cracked open pod. They carry on fighting with the Sky Gliders as the lizard people can't do nothing unless it's close combat, that's why they have lost lots of their kind. The Sky Gliders dart down weaving around the killer objects that the outsiders are sending up, as the sky creatures land on the territory that once was the lizards home.

Max is standing alongside the giant in the dwarf kingdom, as the king dwarf, Minuscule, standing in front of them with his henchmen. Surprisingly for small folks their kings castle is fucking mahoosive. The king wearing a stylish gold armor, his warrior henchmen wearing their black armor.

Minuscule says to the giant "I know why you are here, my men have been briefed on the situation."

The giant says "Good, no time to waste talking, we need to go."

Minuscule says something to one of his henchmen, as they are getting ready to saddle up their ponies.

Estuary's ship stands near ashore, its anchor dug into the seabed to make sure they don't float too far away. Waves crashing into the ships changing imagery. Beside the ship is so many silhouettes pacing towards the land, making the oceans water murky. Waves of Sea Dwellers start emerging from the shallowing oceans close to the ship, as they head onto land one after another. They have all come from their island way out, where their Queen lives, she has been hearing the roars of the Primate king, that's been awoken, to take the earths land because the Sky Gliders Queen was left dead on the battle field.

A Crew member alerts his fellow brothers in arms, to the Sea Dwellers swarming the land.

Estuary's brother says "Well I guess we best take some of these creatures out, cannons at the ready."

As he walks to the ships edge, the Sea Dweller Queen emerges from the water, it's an overgrown Sea Dweller, her subjects protecting her, hanging off from her, her tail smashes into the ship, cracking the shits material, which starts to heal itself.

Estuary's brother says "Bitch."

He takes his sword out, looking down at all of the Sea Dwellers, she doesn't pay any attention to the ship, he just wants to kill the Primate King.

Estuary's brother says "Fire."

Squares like windows on an office building open up. Loaded up with some white, some blue cannon balls seeing the different balls explode out of the cannons. As Estuary's brother along with their crew members, fire their swords towards the swarm. The bombardment hits the Sea Dwellers backs, some lucky as the swords element, get absorbed in their scale, shooting out unlucky for another Sea Dweller, that's hanging off their Queen, gets hit with it instead, all of the salt water inside of the creature, freezes, the Sea Dwellers hardens falling from their Queen. As a white cannon ball hits a Sea Dwellers tail, which is climbing over another sea creature, freezing both their tails together, ice filling up until it's has engulfed them both, as other Sea Dwellers running around the dead or frozen sea creatures.

A Sky Glider is creeping around the old ruins, on the prowl for its next piece of prey, as the creatures walks through the crumbling stone. As the others are fighting amongst themselves, the outsiders are getting the trust of the lizard people, saving their scales from becoming fossils in the ground, for the people from the day'n'age that Max lives in to dig up, to wonder what animal they belonged to. The Sky Glider has stopped to look around the grey stone block room, sniffing the cool breeze, the hint of scent that is coming from the hiding lizard person is close. A pair of chameleon eyes appear from behind the Sky Gliders wings, *hissing* blending into the stonewalls, he releases his tongue latching onto the creatures wing, pulling him backwards before the Sky Glider can react, the lizard person has him in a bear hug, with its mouth opening, strong teeth to start chomping on the back of the fire creatures neck. A spit fire is sent towards the wall before he is killed by the hungry lizard person, that takes another bite which switches the Sky Glider lights out. As the fire smashes into the wall spreading upwards, which will no doubt alert the others battling outside, as a shadow appears walking towards the doorway of this room, while the chameleon lizard person is still eating his winnings, stepping back blending back in with the grey stone fireplace.

Now my friend, it's time for you to be introduced to the larger than life creatures, peering through the bushy green leafs, of a tree trying not to be detected, so 'Shh, please be quiet.' We can see the leafs start trembling with some being up-rooted. Primates running out from the carnage that's about to be displayed, like a pitch invasion at a footie match, at the lower leagues. From the other side shit loads of Sea Dwellers come storming out from in-between the wilderness, like an old school football firm clash. Looking across the battle field, the waves of Primates fighting the Sea Dwellers, like a bomb being dropped from America on to an Syrian village, an uprooted tree explodes in the middle, on top of a flying projectile vomit of ice, that is intended to freeze Primates, but instead freezes the bark also branches to even the leafs are preserved in ice, on the other side, bone darts impacting into the bark, but doesn't last long , smashing onto the ground, wiping out some Sea Dweller, along with some of the other creatures, while shards of ice fly all over the show, as it skips off the ground, rolling through the air, a jagged piece of ice coated bark brakes off, decapitating a Primate.

Max reappears in a city, he looks around to quickly come to terms to where he is or when it is. His sense come to life more expecting to hear a dragon stomping around, releasing fire from within its inner workings, or squawking of ancient birds, with wings flapping, or bricks clattering into other objects from a falling building, but instead everything looks normal like a modern day. He looks around as people are passing him on the street, to see a small shop that he starts approaching while remembering, as he checks his palms, still small streams of blue passing through them, after he opens the door to the small shop.

I just want to take a minute to let you know, that fuck mate, life has got hard through this year of 2019. All I want is to tell you mate appreciate life, because it's short. Fucking hug, kiss also tell your loved ones that you love them because one day they might not be with ya, so to the family that I have lost and still have I Love You All.

Let's see the rest, Max walks into the shop, a few people are looking at the different products to spend money on. Max goes straight forward to the isle that has the newspapers on, he checks the date which is 22-09-2019. Flicking through the pages to yesterday's football scores. He puts his hand in his pocket, to check to see if he has any change to buy the newspaper. It's three days after Mr Bernard Bunsen science experiment went horribly wrong to say the least. He pulls out all the rent money he got from his ashy landlord, taking a twenty out, stuffing the rest back into his pocket.

I'm going to take this time just for a second to let out some stuff from my outlet. First of all I'm sorry to my daughter, I miss you everyday, everyday I'm not by your side but just know I am doing this for us, for our family and your future, hopefully you read this when your older and understand to remember, that just because I wasn't by your side everyday, I have tried to be at least a couple of times a week, that isn't always the case because I haven't seen you in three weeks now, but this always happens, but I have tried to see you over them weeks. I'm not saying your mum is messaging me back the truth, but just know sweetheart, you are my world, your names tattooed on my body, twice. You have my heart, I just want you to know I Love You but I have to make sure, your future is bright while making sure you have the best start, because whenever you get into the bigger version of the world, you have to be more independent and pick the people around you, along with know the person you want to be because I want you to have the resources around, so you can have your own dream.

It's funny now I know why he wrote that song, he had 99 problems, I must of rounded it up to a hundred. Let's get back into the story. Max has reappeared in An Essence Of Time, in front of the giant, that is beside the Sterling Settlement Protectors.

Max asks "Where are Miniature with his men?"

They are walking through the forest, where ahead of them is the commotion of the battle, let's peer through the tree leafs as they dance in front of our vision from the whistling tune of the wind, the battlefield being commanded by the king of the Primates, which can't be seen through the fighting creatures, even the remaining Sky Gliders, have joined to light up the battlefield, as we zoom back to Max.

The giant is responding saying "They are in place around the surrounding forest."

Max asks to the Sterling settlement protectors "You know your names are shortened city names from my time?"

The giant responds saying "Well the elders say there is defining moments now to cement names in history, that's why you're here Max because if this is lost, everything you know will change in your time, even down to the great cities names."

Max says with a chuckle "No pressure then."

Birms with curiosity in his voice asks "So what are our full cities names then."

Cambs adds "I'm glad you asked bro, I was wondering the same."

As the other three nod in agreement, as even the giant is looking on with curiosity.

Max pointing at each one as he responds saying "I'm glad you asked but I would of told you anyway, Cambs is Cambridge, 'best city also football team.' Lon is London the country's capital, Manc is Manchester, 'where is the second best football team is, United, not shitty I mean city.' Birms is Birmingham, 'where my brother lives,' Liver is Liverpool."

Lon says asking "I will take my name being the capital, what about Archie?"

Archie gives out a salute while leaning against a tree.

Max responds saying "His name is to describe what he does, I would call you a archer, someone who shoots with a bow 'n' arrow, but we don't have much use for archers but you guys was important through a lot of history, just an example medieval times but I wasn't around during them times, also now we have guns also knives on the streets."

The giant says "Okay, that's enough of the future history lesson, let's deal with the matter in hand, we can maybe go see the elders later."

Different whistles surrounding them.

There is some rustling to the side of them from the other side....

It's a group of the Rupee warriors, how do I know that, it's because I have met them before but for those who haven't.

"Welcome, I am the leader of the Rupee settlers, Ian."

Lon offers his hand, that Ian shakes, after shaking the rest of the Sterling protectors.

Lon asks "How's it going brother?"

Ian response is to ask back "Can't complain brother apart from leaving the camp to deal with this, how about you?"

Lon responds saying "Pretty much the same bro."

As more of the Rupee campaigners emerge from the surrounding bushes, all of them wearing the last animals fur they last killed, their skin tone is darker than the Sterling Protectors, they all have a red thumb print stretched upwards on their forehead, the main ingredient is vermillion.

No time for everyone to introduce themselves, you know who everyone is.

Let's go check on Mr Bunsen, he is having a weird but wonderful experience, since when we left him getting onto that chopper, that belongs to the Houses of Parliament. That has transformed into a fortress, to protect the rich along with leaders, it's a good thing that there is a fortress but can you see these guys rebuilding the city's capital after all this destruction, so if all goes to shit, the working class will die but at least there will be people with money left behind to do what in our absence, well they would have shit loads to do after food shortage, go out to hunt to get their own prey instead of having their butlers bring it to them, that is something I would go pay money to watch, see them trying to survive in a place where money doesn't mean nothing, along with avoiding becoming prey. well if the first story is correct I would be watching it from the after life, if anything it should be good for a laugh.

Anyway, Mr Bunsen is walking down a corridor of the Houses of Parliament, he is pushing a trolley with his global time machine on, he is being escorted to a underground lab by the prime minister, Boris, they are discussing a couple of things while turning into a doorway.

Before we get back to the battle, that is near temperature, just a few more minutes to get her up to boiling, as the flames flicker up the side of my saucepan, half owner of the Fuego food truck cooking up a treat for yourselves.

Inferno is helping up Stoner from the ground, as a torn scorched chunk of Sky Gliders meaty flesh, still pulsating beside. Stoner on his feet, walking alongside Inferno back to the other two.

Stoner says "Cheers for having my back brother."

Inferno putting his sword back, offering his hand which Stoner slaps, as they bump fists. A mixture of Sky Gliders along with lizard people, engulfed in the elements that the outsiders possess, a stone figure standing in between flames, the stone looking like a influential figure on Mount Rushmore, but that's not from them stone carvers, that would be the outcome of Stoners craftsmanship, them flames on the other hand should be without saying the handy work of Inferno also the once alive Sky Gliders. As they both walk up to, Neon, Estuary alongside Glizzie, that is growing in numbers because the surviving lizard people joining. Glizzie is the first to show his appreciation to the outsiders, while the congratulations are happening, all of them totally unaware there is a bow, resting on top of a tree trunk, loading with an arrow aiming, in the crosshairs is the dominant LP, Glizzie. Like a resting black leopard laying on a tree trunk, a Franc settlement archer, waiting for a goldfinches tune to fire, along with the others waiting up the surrounding trees, for the same bird call. The archer looking down to see the settlement leader, Witzer alongside his younger brother Swiss, walking underneath towards the forest clearing, wearing their red armors with their countries crest on the front along with shields, their archers darkly dressed differently, because of their unique methods of traveling through the bushes above. You wouldn't be able to see but look closely, you might.

Inferno is brushing himself down, as he is looking at Glizzie with the forest clearing behind him, through around a couple of LPs heads, you can see it.

Neon asks "So how did you lot come about? Like what's your evolution?"

Stoner adds "I was wondering the same because I am sure a lizard, didn't make wonderful love with a woman then one of you's popped out, nine months later."

Glizzie chuckles as he responds saying "No that didn't happen, we was sent here from our planet, many moons ago."

In the distance the archer is making his way out of the tree, while Glizzie continues to say "A handful was sent here to inspect this world because, they didn't want to send anyone of importance, they sent us, convicts."

Movements behind as Glizzie continues to ask "How did you get here because you're outsiders?"

Inferno responds asking "Pretty much the same apart from we are not convicts, we are our worlds protectors, how long have you been here?

Glizzie responds saying "Fuck knows, we don't have time but what I do know is we have seen a lot of moons pass to sun rises."

Stoner responds saying "I bet your people have forgotten about you guys, dude."

Inferno responds asking "Dude?"

Glizzie adds in "I am glad you asked, I don't know what it means."

Stoner responds saying "It's a word from my language, it's like saying bro."

Neon responds asking "Oh so like mate?"

Inferno responds saying "Nice, I like both...."

Inferno's sentence is cut short by Witzer's short sword tip, digging into Glizzie's neck, one push it would slice through his jugular. The outsiders, back away at the same time, releasing their weapons from their holsters.

Estuary orders "You don't wanna be another burning body on this land, friend."

As the outsiders eyes flickering around to see, Swiss is pointing his sword at the back of Glizzie's right hand man, Meleon. Franc settlement's archers lined up ready to unleash arrows like rainfall.

Witzer laughs after says "I just wanted to see your faces."

After he puts his sword back, as he puts his arm around Glizzie, Witzer's men put their swords away.

Glizzie asks "How are you brother? Still pulling pranks I see."

Witzer response is to put his hands up while saying "Well you know a leopard don't change his spots bro."

Glizzie responds saying "Well I know you never will bro, we have a strong friendship with all of the different settlements, sat with them within their kingdoms, eating meals beside their wives also kids. We have saved their people along with stood beside during battles."

Witzer responds saying "Well now we have another battle, so let's wrap this up before we miss it."

As they start walking towards the echoing Primate roars, while introducing each other.

Zarah still on ground level giving people shelter, as she opens her front door, as she waves a couple in from the street, while shouting "Quickly, come over here!"

As chaos still runs riot on the streets, while Max is still in this earths historical moment that will define today, history always runs parallel to the future. Over the shoulder of Zarah is the kettle boiling, with a couple of cups in front, you can design your own cup that has a spoon in, but mine is a Fuego one.

As the couple are walking into, past Zarah, that is asking "Do you want a drink?"

The woman's voice shaking while she responds saying "Yes please...."

Zarah shuts her front door.

Lookin both ways, their right nothing is going on apart from the army, combing down the street. They're looking left a whole different story of course, two men in black suits, one of the men are bald, as they cross the road walking towards Zarah's front door, with their government car behind them. Their eyes flickering around the carnage that is fully unleashed, with bullets flying from the army, that is holding its own against a couple of creatures, apart from the soldier laying on the ground, with a Redcap, that is currently soaking his cap in the bloody soldiers guts, the Redcaps blood dripping scythe leaning over his small shoulder, after he puts his hat back on, strands of insides splashing on the Redcaps forehead, along with bloody droplets, some dripping out of his eyebrows.

As the lone Redcap runs towards another soldier, that is looking in the opposite direction. Flickering to a Centaur that is shooting a arrow but the creature is quickly gunned down, while in the background, you can see the solider gun butt the Redcap after shoots him, as they carry on sweeping down the road, still fighting more of the creatures on their way, while one of the government men knocks on her front door, a soldier bends down taking his fallen brothers dog tags, from around his neck after he runs back into his position, within the sweeping formation while shoving them in his pocket. But they are walking towards a SMW, which is actually good because they have never killed a human, well not intentionally anyway. The SMW has control of a Redcap, gripping ahold of the creatures bloody cap his brain within, still attached to the creatures small body, intestines slipping off from the cap, splattering onto the road.

Now it's time for the Fuego chef to serve, cutlery at the ready, view how the food magician, magically displays his art like paintings hanging in a gallery, as people observe, discussions begin as it passes through them.

Through the eyes of the Primate king, we observe the battlefield. Sky Gliders looking tiny compared, swatting away them creatures from eye sight, some get squashed in the hands leathery but scarred palm, like flies in a swatter, rubbing them against the fur that's surrounding his left thigh, squashed Sky Gliders fall to the ground. Seeing a Sky Glider trapped within one of the many scars, taking him out by his wings, flinging the creature to one side. Looking past the palm, crowded Primates, protecting, with some dead Sky Gliders to the side, that got too close to the Primate King. Looking slowly up, seeing across the whole battlefield, eyes flickering from blood being spilt on the mud below, to a Sky Gliders with its wings flapping, mid-air, spit fire bolting out from the creatures mouth. Flickering past the settlement protectors that's defending himself from the Sky Gliders fire, until his eyes stop on Max, that has just froze a Primate by using his Gifted Hands. Fire explodes around a Sky Gliders body, descending back to the earth below, as Max, turns to catch the Primate King watching him, as the flaming Sky Gliders, wings flapping trying to extinguish but can't as its body meets the mud behind, Max starts running faster obliterating everything to get to make sure the future is safe, the only thing that will secure that is, slaying the Primate King.

Max running towards the Primate King, freezing along with blazing enemies along his way. The giant on the other hand had to find a different route, undetected, because running through the battlefield wouldn't of been a wise move, he would of squashed everything, including the people he is sworn to protect. Before he makes it to the Primate King, he is stopped by a couple of Sea Dwellers, as he is trying to be swift in killing them off, he notices in the distance, Queen Sea Dweller is roaming on earths land, which hasn't happened in about seven years, his ancient battle-axe splitting a Sea Dweller in two, halves slump to the ground, insides spilling out. Another Sea Dweller is quickly made lifeless before the creature can get any shot off, the giant treating him like a jam doughnut, squashing, blood spurting out from every orifice, as he stamps on another, but before he can get the jump on the Primate King, or the Sea Dweller Queen, some Primates come to take on the giant.

The Primate king standing tall, watching over the battlefield. Compared to the king some measly Sky Gliders try to attack from behind, something you might not know is that the Primates tails are their defense mechanism, so if they sense danger it will naturally protect, by the time I have just explained a vital part of the creature inner workings, a bone dart has turnt their brains off, deadeye with the aiming. The

Sea Dwelling Queen lunges out from the surrounding forest, latching onto the Primate King. As he falls, she is squeezing her claws tighter into him, but his clenched fist connects onto her body. Squashing everything on impact with the ground, trees snapped, creatures bones broke flattened on impact, lucky there wasn't any humans close. The Queen is rolling off as the king is making his way back to his feet, pulling broken branches out from his rib area, blood spurts, but his fur catches most of his blood. The Primate king roars, as Max is ready to capture the overgrown Primitive king, fingers ready to get waved, a blue light engulfs to flash around Max, disappearing to be needed somewhere else.

While they all fight it out, let's go see what Mr Bunsen is doing, three men sitting at a table, in different clothing, scanning through their big brothers on the streets, they have their backs to the room, but there is a big screen in front of them. As the middle one is clicking to typing, to watching while the other two either side, their eyes scanning some live cctv, as they are diverting some facilities on ground levels, to where it is needed. As Boris's voice comes from behind the three of them, as he is brainfart... brain storming with these scientists that was on the chopper with Bernard, that is behind them, his global time machine split in two as he is working on the inside.

Inside the Sterling Settlement, Coven, Leist alongside Gordon are standing at the settlements bonfire, roasting some Sea Dweller meat, on the massive skewer.
Gordon holding the skewer, rotating it while he asks "How do you think the guys are..."
He is instantly interrupted by some ruckus coming from outside the settlements entrance. By the looks of it the Primates have come to disturb the peace. Leist alongside Coven are off to find out what is causing the commotion while

Gordon lays the skewer on the floor after grabs his sword off from under his preparation station.

They turn up to see the guards holding off the Primates from entering the settlement. Their fueling pumping station in the distance beside their airplane, that took them ages to build, they still have the blueprints which will come in handy for other settlements, when Neon crashed here in the first book, go buy it! It is heavily guarded because we wouldn't want any of the creatures to come along to destroy all the Sterling settlements hard work. Settlement archers posted on top of the entrances stone pillars, arrows raining down towards the Primates, that are trying to weaken the settlements defenses.

Max appears in a blue flash, beside a Primate they both look at each other, the creature looks startled at the fact, Max just appeared but it works in Max's favor because he is quick to flip the creature the bird, flames spew out like a dormant volcano finally erupting. As he starts moving towards the entrance, helping his fellow Sterling people as shakes within the grounds surface get closer. Max has got to avoid running onto a arrow, as they whiz over heads. A Primate with his tail poised to let a couple of bone darts hit the back of Max, from a camouflaged position the creature thinks its being sneaky within the bushes, rubbing its hands as the bone dart is loaded into his tails center. While Max freezes a Primate to his left, setting another alight to his right, a arrow flies over the top of his head, he must of felt the wood graze his hair, lucky he isn't taller, as another arrow flies over but on a higher level, Max checking over his shoulder to see the first arrow, knock a flying bone dart off course, because it was on course to kill Max by entering through the back of his head, the second arrow like a juggernaut through the air, penetrates through the hiding Primate, through where they believe their pineal eye is, Max puts his thumb up to archers, they nod back, clutching their left chest side as a mark of respect. As the small wave of

Primates have been defeated, they can breathe easily but for how long.

Max being joined by the outsiders, the LPs which are alongside the Franc settlement protectors. After they have all introduced themselves apart from the ones which already know each other.

Max while pointing asks Coven "Bro, is that an airplane I see over there?"

Coven responds "Yes, we built it with the help from Neon along with the other outsiders."

"LOOK!" Bellows out from an archer above as he points to the loud ruffling trees like someone ruffing your hair, Max's eyes follows the path that comes out from settlement, that he will be born into, a long way into the future, the path runs beside a stream, with some different type of fish swimming in what they call their settlement, where the stream curves, the path is engulfed by the forest. Trees are becoming quickly flattened as you can see the Primate Kings head bobbing, but seems to be in a rush as he emerges from the forest engulfed pathway.

Everyone at the settlements entrance, withdrawing their weapons out of their holsters. One of the archers pulling back on a loaded arrow, but is quickly stopped by Leist shouting up "Not yet!"

Max hoping the Giant or at least the other Sterling settlement protectors are the next to emerge to keep the Primate king entertained but it is....

WHOP-EESH! as the Queen Sea Dwellers tail cracks on the King's hairy back, his face winces in pain which soon turns to anger, as she tries to crack her tail again, like a whip being cracked onto a horses rear at the grand national.

Her tail whips back ready to strike again, but lucky for the Primate king, that manages to spin around to grab ahold of her tail before it splits his back again, the king isn't as stupid as he looks because knowing her defense mechanism, he shoves her own tail through one of her scales, his mounting of a back now facing the Sterling settlement, you can see the wound left behind, leaking with blood, mixing with the many strands of brown hairs. The Queen not even matching the height of the king but still trying to get at his throat while she is trying to remover her tail from within herself, which has really pissed her off by the way. She is going to send a projectile of ice up at him, but he isn't in the mood for some stuck in the mud, big up yourself if you remember playing that as a youngster, his fist connects on her jaw, swinging the projectile vomit of ice at a tree. I'm sure you can guess the tree has become the victim of stuck in the mud. The Primate Kings hand seems to be cut up from the Queen Sea Dwellers sharp tail along with teeth. While the two boss creatures fight it out.

Glizzie asks Max "Have you seen a Samarium Wolfram yet? I mean like here or in your day'n'age?"

Max responds asking "Not yet, what do they look like?"

Coven responds asking to Glizzie "Is that what you call them? We call them 'SMW.'

Glizzie nods in agreement Max states "Well I still would like to know what they look like or do."

Coven responds saying "You will know when you see one, they float off the ground, there is some places on this earth we haven't been to because it's under their control also we haven't found a way of defeating them."

Witzer responds "If you believe the stories, I haven't seen one."

Glizzie responds saying "I thought I see one once but didn't want it to see me, so I didn't stick around."

Max responds asking "So they are just stories? Was they past down from your elders?"

Coven nods in agreement, we have already seen one or two if you remember, so has Max but he didn't know the name of it. While the Giant has emerged from the paths clearing, his ancient battle axe blocking his face from bone darts along with icicles being spewed out by the Sea Dweller Queen, the bone darts on the other hand, are not coming from the king but instead his subjects, as she turns her attention to the Primate King, with her tail stuck but slowly wriggling free, as more creatures start emerging from the forest, still fighting from the battlefield, all the surrounding settlements are joining in, their protectors were close by, when they heard the primitive roaring. On that note the Sea Dweller Queen has drawn blood, from the Primate King, on her second bite at his shin on his right leg, he bends down to grab her but she is too quick, ripping another chunk, his hairs still attached, some getting stuck in her teeth, sometimes you gotta trim. But now he is pissed off, starting to stamp with his other leg, it's like the first type of 'Whack-A-Mole.' While a soaking Sky Glider comes from behind the Giants legs, the sky's above start to darken, rain pours from the heavens above, rumbling overpowers the roars of the royal creatures fighting one another, as lightning rolls across the sky above, mixing into the dark clouds, a bolt strikes down, onto the now wet electrocuting Sky Glider, *X-Ray.* You can see strands of lightning passing through, down the shaking Sky Gliders body, can you see his organs being electrocuted? His heart going into cardiac arrest from the bolts voltage. Cambs alongside Lon come out from the forest, pointing their swords at the Sky Glider, that is shaking on the battles ground, soon to be dead, falling to the ground, steaming as the rain, thunder also lightning suddenly stop until the next time. Cambs goes to fight a Primate while Lon helps by setting them up first, for Cambs to strike down. Manc's stone rubble lay scattered around the battlefield, dead creatures lay beneath them. Birms standing in front of the Giant, he sees the Sea Dweller, in which Manc is pointing his sword at, they both shoot their sword at the same time, their elements mix, on route, hitting the unbeknown sea creatures body, a grey cloud musters above, starting to rain down shards of stone, getting bigger as time passes, the creature defense mechanism comes in handy, when the shards are small but as they get bigger not so much, a shard the size of the cloud, splits the Sea Dweller in two. Birms points his sword at a Primate, that has just been set alight by Livers sword, a tornado forms around the flaming Primate, eventually shredding it to pieces, when the tornado clears, it just leaves a pile of scorched dismembered Primate limbs, flames still flicking off, from

the Fuego meat. The giant still fighting off the Sky Gliders, their spitfires just exploding on the giants arms but not causing any damage, just a burnt patches that can be washed off. A massive bone dart sent from the Primate King, stabbing into the ground, through the Sea Dwellers tails hoop, before she can dislodge her tail from inside herself , but it is loosening the bone dart sticking out from the blood soaked soil, from her whipping side to side. *Slow time.* The Giants ancient axe diagonally slices, through her mid-section, snapping through her scales, until it glides through her leathery skin, to bones. Clinking off the bone dart, her tail gets chopped into, another couple of whacks with the axe to guarantee the Sea Dwellers Queen's death. All the fighting suddenly ceases, as her last noises are of whining. All of the Sea Dweller Queen's children are quick to leave the battlefield, going across the fielded area towards the ocean, most probably back to their island. Max is getting his hands ready to shoot at the Primate King, which is standing nearly toe to toe with the Giant. As the Sky Gliders are pretty much extinct by the end of this battle, the remaining few fly off in surrender. The king roars down at his Primates, as they start to scurry away, jumping off all the dead creatures around, as Cambs is doing a head count, all of the Sterling settlement residency is watching on, some peaking over the walls. The Primate King beats his chest, while the Giant dropping his axes wooden handle, after beating his chest, a few seconds then they stop, bowing their heads, after the Primate King carries on going forward, he looks at Max, that knows he could heal the primitive creatures wounds but can also cause them, the primitive kings open wounds are still leaking blood. Before anything else happens Max disappears into the blue mist.

Max reappears in front of his flats rundown apartment complex, his senses come back to focus, waiting to hear the crackle of fire or buildings collapsing or creatures running wild but instead he sees normal life, hearing horns honking from traffic building up, buildings standing tall. Max walks down the street, to a bookies, before he enters he checks his pocket, pulling out the future newspaper from his back pocket, along with the money he took from his landlord. He goes in to place a certain bet, for tomorrow's football matches, what's the betting he gets all the scores correct, as for the rest such as Mr Bunsen also Boris well they are still alive.

The children of the Sterling settlement protectors sitting on logs, listening to this story being told by Lon also Cambs.
One of the kids asks "Why didn't the Giant fight the Primate King?"
Lon's father Big Ben answers that by saying "Now that is a story for me to tell you youngsters... ."

Until next time my friend, salute... .

I finished this story during the co-vid 19 lockdown, if there is anything I have learnt over the last few years, having to attend many funerals, seeing my mum lay in that hospital bed, not believing she died so young, still filled with so much life along with love, then a few months later going through it all again with my lady's father, a strong man suffocating to death after having a heart attack at home, thinking that has to be the worst way to go out along with being so young only 46 but I think my mum just needed company, she was only 47. That was only two deaths out of seven I went through last year. I couldn't break down, I had to be strong for my brothers also my lady, I am glad I didn't because I could of fucked my whole life, thankful to the strength inside, which is what everyone needs now, we will get through this as nations unite together, no matter the culture or shade of skin, we are all humans. Peace to everyone that have lost their life to this along with the families of this. Stay safe out there, don't forget to wash your hands for 20 seconds also keep your distance, also be kind to each other especially the elderly, don't forget to take care of them, especially your grandparents because they took care of your parents also they have so much wisdom to teach to future generations, so we don't have to be idiots, intelligence lasts forever.

Stand Beside Me

It is time for us to step into this visual display

A dark stormy evening has risen, thunder rumbling in the distance with rain pouring, deep within a forest in the middle of nowhere. A dark glistening saloon car engine turning filling the gaps between the rumbling thundering, rays of car lights, lighting up the forest surface, a deep hole that has nearly been dug, two occupied twitching bodybags lay parallel, muffled noises come from within both of them, a small oxygen hole at the feet of each bodybag. Some mud being flung out, after a couple of times, followed by a muddy shovel, that lands on top of the pile of wet soil. The Fellow Gent George emerges from the grave, he pulls up a muddy wooden ladder from within the grave. He takes his blue latex gloves off, chucking them into the hole, just to fix his slicked back black hair.

George shouts at the wiggling bodybags, "Oh be quiet! At least you two can fuck in peace In the afterlife, for being a cheating bitch to your husband, personally I would of just shot you both to be done with it, but the contract said for you to suffer Kate!"

He shifts both of the body bags into the grave, as the first thumps into the muddy bottom, enough to take the air out of his lungs, Kate follows him, thumping on top of him, the muffle cries for help stop, now just the gasping for air, raindrops splashing on the bodies black plastic coating. George walks over to the mud pile, picking up the shovel as he is shoveling mud back into the grave.

We touch down in a botanical garden, a couple holding hands walking along the path, both are dressed in casual clothes, looking at the different flowers, such beauty with each different type also shades. Personally I sneeze shit loads if I have flowers in my home, but my lady loves them, so I put up with It, sometimes. A darkish blue Stylish suited Fellow Gent is walking towards the couple, that are pointing at the flowers, to the side is a duck pond, with ducks swimming in, quacking to each-other, a swan is swimming around like she owns the pond but that's In the distance. The lady bends down while hooking a strand of her chestnut hair, over her ear, to sniff a blossoming Cherry flower.

The Fellow Gent stops the couple, grabbing ahold of the woman's arm, not tightly but enough for her to be startled.

The Fellow Gent says "Gemma, we need to talk, I am George, it is about your father also his grandson, Luke."

Before Gemma can respond, her fella pipes up asking, "Err, can I help you mate?"

George *responds saying "I don't believe I was talking to you, mate. It is Gemma, I need to speak with, so stand aside or be seated here."*

George continues to say to the lady "Let's take a walk to talk."

Gemma nods after tells her fella Neil "It will be fine, stay here."

They kiss each other a few times while George is whistling.

George is walking alongside Gemma on a path, with several types of flower beds on the right side. On the left side is a lush green field, with other couples along with families walking about, with trees scattered around, wooden benches are around the small duck pond.

Gemma asks "How do you know my name?"

George responds saying "Your father is the head of The Fellow Gents. As you know, you are his only child, he also knows you have a son called Luke. Now he hasn't forgotten his grandson, but being a respected head for mafia firms, who can't get their hands dirty over a contract, they hire us to do it, he didn't want to put you two in harms way."

George suddenly stops in his tracks, pulling something from inside his jacket, to extend it to something behind them, following his arm to his hand, that is gripping his gun, trigger finger poised to strike. On the side of his gun Is the words, etched In 'Bring you to silence.' It Is pointing at Neil, which has been following them.

George says "Listen, I will tell you this once don't follow me because I can put you down then get away before anyone can sneeze."

Gemma says to Neil "Don't follow, everything will be fine."

Neil nods as he backs away putting his hands up, George retreats his gun back into its holster, after he proceeds walking with Gemma to a bench around the duck pond.

They both sit at the duck pond, while a few other people are feeding the floating animals.

George says "As I was saying, he didn't want to put you two In harms way, Neil on the other hand he doesn't give two shits about, if he wanted him buried he would have been in the woods digging his own grave, but he sees how happy you are so he respects that."

Gemma responds asking "I understand that, but why send you to tell me all of this?"

George responds saying "I am the only one he fully trusts, also everything he does is under the watchful eyes of the people who want to bury him. He feels it's time because something is going to happen involving him. So he wants his daughter also grandson to be taken care of.

Gemma responds saying defensively "He is being taken care of by me."

George responds saying "He knows you're a good mother, full of love, he has asked me to to tell you if you could tell Luke, that he loves him everyday please."

Gemma nods as she responds saying "I will, just tell him from me to keep himself safe please."

George responds saying "Anyway I must go, oh yes before I do. This Is just for yourself also Luke, open it when you get in."

George rummaging around in a pocket inside his suit jacket, pulling a large brown package, he passes it to her. Gemma takes it from him after turns to put the package In her handbag. She turns back to ask him a question but George has already made his leave, nowhere to be seen as she stands up looking around.

Some years have passed, a sad day is on The Fellow Gents. I'm sure they have dug to put many people in their graves but it Is harder when it's someone you love. George is wearing a black suit, he has grown a full beard since the last time we saw him, some grey hairs running through his dark beard. As he stands at a graveside on the day of the funeral of Gemmas father, also the head of The Fellow Gents. She is opposite from George, Gemma dressed in a black dress, standing behind a young man which is Luke, dressed in a black suit, he is clean shaven. Gemma has her hands on his shoulders, George looking at Gemma which has tears forming a path down her cheeks. There are mobsters all dressed in black suits around the grave, four of them lowering the coffin with ropes, as the priest is doing their god speech, maybe unaware of the type of person, they are making peace with god on their behalf. The other mobsters have their heads bowed with their hand holding the other one in front of themselves. The priest gives a box full of dirt to Gemma, she takes some throwing it on the coffin below, which has some single roses scattered on his dark wooden overcoat. after he gives it to Luke which throws mud Into his grandfathers grave, the box is offered to others which are in attendance. George does the Jesus Cross on himself with his right index finger, after puts his shades on as he walks away.

After the funeral, George Is speaking with some mafia heads. As he notices Gemma with Luke walking towards a luxury black funeral limo, George takes his shades off putting them away.
George says "I will speak to you lot later."
He leaves them to walk towards Gemma which makes eye contact with George so she stops to speak with him.
George says "I wish we could of met under better circumstances, he didn't die for no reason I will make sure of that."

Gemma sympathy smiles at George as he Is offering his hand for Luke to shake, but he isn't going to shake his hand Instead...

He asks "Who the fuck is you?"

George puts his hand back into his trouser pocket while Gemma puts her arm around Liam to comfort him.

George says "I was a close friend of your grandfather, well I am still am."

Luke responds with some venom in his voice "He isn't my grandad, I never fucking see him."

Gemma rubs Luke's back to try comfort him while George says "I know but he is still your grandad mate, I wish I could tell you why he was never around, but it doesn't mean he didn't care for you or love you both, or even want to spend time with you because he did.

Luke nods as George Is noticing the resemblance in Luke to his grandfather.

George passes him a key after says "This may help you understand."

After he smiles at both of them, he walks away towards his fancy red sports car. Luke looks down to the key It has an address engraved on the key ring.

Later that day, George wearing a different suit, a three piece dark blue pinstripes, with a dark blue shirt, red tie. He is walking through a corridor of a run down building, past a room full of green plants that will get you higher, than Bob Marleys irises was. A Shirtless Latino guy, covered In tattoos taking buds off one of the many plants. In the doorless rotting doorway a machine gun leans up against the doorframe. He carries on walking down the corridor towards the door at the end, dirty walls with peeling off wallpaper. He takes a peep Into another room which is full of topless Latino women, tits out not In their bras mate, some are counting money, at a decrepit brown table, in the kitchen area same type of women wearing white masks, with jugs out nipples hard, they are scooping white powder Into brown packaging. George carries on walking, pleasurable moaning becomes more apparent, as he takes a peek into the last open room, just before he gets to the door he needs, he sees a naked woman riding a guy on a bed, she is facing George, her boobs bouncing while she is rubbing her clit, she winks at George as he passes, to his destination. A rotting brown door, he puts his ear to the wood, to hear a slight gagging noise, that's when he opens....

In front of George is a hefty business man, that runs all the things George has just walked past. His name is Tomas, he Is wearing a grey suit, sitting at a desk, but not for much longer because for a big guy he Is quick to get up.

Angrily asking "Who the fuck are you?"

To the side, behind him is a gaping window, that has had its glass smashed in, to the side of that Is where Tomas's henchman in a blue suit is gasping for air, because of a Fellow Gent, called Flames, is strangling him with cheese wire. Now the reason why he is called Flames is simple really, he likes to burn shit down, but also he wears a mask with flames on when he's doing it, burning shit down that is, not having sex, well he might who knows. George closes the door, a peep hole In the middle of the door.

George asks "Evening all, hows it going Flames?"

Flames nods in response, he is dressed all In black with black shades on.

George says "Forgot your not much of a talker, any who, listen Tomas shut your lard ass up, also while you're at it sit down before you bust a blood vessel."

Tomas with face like thunder slowly sits down, while George walks over to a wooden chair, that is in front of a crumbling wall, grabbing ahold of It.

George says to Flames "You can drop him now bro."

George sits opposite Tomas at the wooden desk, while Flames swings the struggling purple faced henchman out of the window.

George smiles while saying "Not what I had in mind."

Hearing the henchman gasp screaming after splat, pedestrians screaming at the man that just splattered onto the pavement.

Tomas asks angrily, I mean that anger, spits flings from his mouth, "Why the fuck did you do that!?"

Flames walks over to Tomas as he pulls his shades down to the top of his nose, he puts his finger to his lips after going "Shhhh."

orangey tint in Flames eyes, he pushes his shades back.

George says "Thank you Flames, now let me get to the real reason why I am here, as you may of heard the boss of The Fellow Gents was killed."

Tomas getting a bit fidgety, responds saying "Yes, so I know nothing about it."

George responds asking "Don't you hate people who lie Flames?"

He nods as Tomas starts to get even more fidgety, chins wriggling as he is trying to get up but is stopped by the right hand of Flames on his shoulder.

Tomas says "Even if I did know something, you know I can't talk."

George says "Well this isn't getting me nowhere fast."

He pulls two un-silenced guns from their holsters, inside his suit jacket, he shoots Tomas twice, one in his chest where his heart Is, the other between his eyes, he slumps over the desk, blood seeping all over the desk, soaking Into the scattered papers on the desk, trickling down to the floor below.

George just about to say something, but a bullet wizzes past their heads through the room, through the peep hole in the door, hitting the oncoming topless Latino man with hid machine gun, right between his eyes. His body has soon become lifeless, thudding the ground. The panicking screams of the topless ladies echoes through the building, as they start to flee the scene, George goes to the window putting his thumb up to a black figure on a rooftop opposite, which is packing their things up.

George says "Come on, let's look to see if there Is anything that will help us."

They start to look around the desk, opening the draws, shuffling through the loose papers, the ones that are still readable, not blood soaked. Tomas's lifeless body lets off gas, a stinky one at that.

Luke gets off from a public bus, he would of drove but you know it's fucking expensive just to park for a day In any cities centre, cheaper to get a day rider. Luke turns left, dodging around the people waiting for buses or shopping, as he walk past a clothing shops window display, with three stylish mannequins, the fourth Is getting sorted out by a lady, which I would presume works there, Luke catches her eye, they smile at each other, he turns crossing the road, between two bus stops, he puts his hand up as a thanks to a slowing taxi, the driver puts his index finger up, his hands on the steering wheel. He walks around the corner on the other side of the street, a homeless person sitting outside the bank, a scraggy fella, Luke gives him the change from the day rider.

The fella says "Thank You."

Luke taps the key within his hand while taking a deep breath, he Is double checking the address of the bank with the homeless person. Diverse types of people walking around, going about their business most of them wearing suits, bankers, Im sure some of them are what rhymes with bankers, snobby ones. A number three bus stops at Its correct bus stop, as a number two along with one bus pull away from their bus stops, after picking up people.

He says "Thank You" to the homeless man, Luke walks into the bank .

Luke standing in a room full of numbered metal bank deposit boxes, a security guard standing guard out of the room, Luke is the only person within the room, there Is a wooden table with a single chair, tucked underneath. He goes to the number 19 that's been etched on to the key, tries the key but it doesn't work, he decides to add 19 with the address number which is 17, in total it's 36. Quick maths for ya. So he finds that number to try the key, the metal slated door, opens, if the metal box didn't open, I would presume he would of tried seventeen. He slides out the box, placing it on the table, sitting down on the chair to sieve through the contents. There Is a credit card, with Luke's name on, with a transparent piece of paper, you know the ones you get sent from the bank, It tells you the cards pin, yeah that one, his is telling him the pin for his card, I won't tell you his pin though. A white envelope is inside the box with his name scribbled on the front, in the middle. There is also two keys inside the box, attached to each other. Luke grabs ahold of the envelope, opening it up to read the letter inside. We are gong to leave him there reading.

Within the letter another address for Luke to visit but before he goes there, he Is standing outside of the bank he was just in, in front of a whole in the wall, or for those who don't know that expression, a cash point. Luke's checking the balance on his new card, he types in the pin while double checking with the slice of pin coded paper. He clicks the balance button, the amount exceeds having It In number form on the screen instead it just states the amount In words. He turns seeing a old lady, walking with a stroller thing, you know the ones that old folks put their shopping in. His ecstatic behavior nearly gives her a cardiac arrest.

He asks her "My darling, do you mind just double checking what that says?"

While she puts her glasses on, shaking a little while she gets them out of her handbag, the cashpoint beeps, asking on the screen "Do you need more time?" Luke obviously clicks more time, the balance comes back up on the screen, the same as before. The old lady looks at the screen, now with her glasses on.

She is shocked while she responds "10 million, 7 hundred thousand."

Luke laughing like a giddy kid, while responding "That is what I thought it said, just didn't believe my eyes."

The machine beeps again, this time Luke's presses 'No' to the machines request to give more time, he takes his card, kissing the old lady on the cheek.

Luke says "Thank you, enjoy your day my dear."

The old lady smiles, as she carries on with her journey through the city's center, Luke on the other hand goes back into the bank to get some of that money out, It would be rude not to use It.

The cafés door opens which causes the bell above to ring, a few of the local café dwellers heads turn to see, George walks through the doorway, wearing the same suit as before. Some people sitting around, mainly builders, eating breakfast, can't beat a good old café full English mate, especially after a hangover or arriving in a different city. He walks around the tables to the counter, looking through a doorway, to a chunky short fella, In grubby whites, cooking breakfast stuff on a flat top grill, bacon along with sausages sizzling away, as he cracks a couple of eggs onto the flat top grill, they are start spluttering like a person who can't get their words out.

The cook puts his index finger up as he shouts through to George, "One moment mate!"

George with a raised voice responds "I just want a coffee chef!"

The cook with spatula in hand, flipping the eggs as well as tending to the rest of the breakfast, takes a peak at the person that wants the coffee.

"Oh it's you Georgie, help yourself I thought it was you by your voice!"

George walks around the counter as he starts making his coffee.

George responds asking "How's business chef!?"

"It's been a nice week so far." He doesn't shout through because he is leaving the kitchen with two other full English breakfasts in his hands, maneuvering around the the counter too tables to two builders, wearing hi-vis vests, that are chatting amongst themselves while drinking their tea's.

At the same time they both say, "Thank you chef."

While walking away the chef responds "You're welcome lads."

Chef walks back towards the kitchen to finish off the other breakfasts.

While George Is stirring his coffee, he rummages around in his trouser pocket, placing a fiver in the chefs hand, as they shake. George says "Don't worry about giving me the change, I will have another coffee after this one."

The chef responds saying "Just let me know when Georgie."

Chef grabs his cold tea from beside the till, after walks back Into the the kitchen, while George takes a sip of his coffee, as he walks over to a table in the center of the café to carry on with business, chef will come to chat with George after he is finished them breakfasts.

Luke walks out of the bank, he was allowed to withdraw one thousand five hundred quid, sitting down beside the homeless man.

Luke asks "How did you become homeless my man?"

The homeless man with a crooked nose, most probably from many fights trying to survive being swallowed up by the streets, wanting to avoid being another John Doe on the Leichendiener table, if your not sure what Leichendiener means, let me educate ya a little, it means corpse servant or someone that's a doctor of a morgue, it's a German word, google Is a handy tool to have mate.

The homeless man responds "My name Is Liam, I think I was about twenty two when I become homeless, this country along with its system is ass backwards, I was aspiring boxer until I ran into some bad men, that wanted me to throw a fight, that I wish I had because I didn't go down In the sixth round Instead I knocked the guy out in round two, they come after me, when I put a few of their henchmen in hospital, they decided to kill my parents along with sister, so I had to flea my city I come here with barely two coins to rub together, no place to stay I went to the council, well they are about as helpful as filling a chocolate tea pot with hot water."

Luke responds saying "That is madness, I can Imagine you couldn't even go to their funerals, I am Luke by the way."

Liam responds "Nah if I did I would of got kidnapped then killed, I am sure they got a paupers send off."

Luke responds asking "That is sad mate, do you miss boxing?"

Liam responds "Of course, It has helped me being on the streets In so many ways, I don't smoke or drink apart from water on occasion someone gives me a fizzy bottle as a handout, so I save money there also when other homeless people come to take your sleeping spot, I can fight them off, it's funny though I used to knock men out in the ring fairly quick but these fuckers take a bit longer, that's how I got this nose, it wasn't crooked before street life."

Luke responds asking "Yeah to be a boxer you have to be well disciplined. Listen if I give you this, you will invest it wisely."

Liam responds "Well If there is one thing I have always learnt, invest in yourself."

Luke pulls out five hundred quid from his pocket, passing it to Liam, that can't believe this is happening."

Liam stammers in shock as he says "Thank you, you are a saint."

Luke says "I hope this will help you a little, next time I see you I hope you're in a better position Liam."

They both stand up, Liam hugs him tightly, Luke hugs him back.

George still sitting in the café, facing the window in the center of the room, so he can see the people passing, going about their business, mainly doing shopping in the city's center. The chef behind him doing little bits of cleaning, waiting for customers to come or go, a few tables still taken up by builders. Now you might be wondering or you won't be, but George isn't just a regular here, The Fellow Gents own this café, all five members get ten percent of the earnings, the other fifty percent gets reinvested into the café. The Fellow Gent members are of course George, Flames, Carver, Pinpoint last but not least is Knuckles.

The bell rings as the café door opens, Mr Carver walks In. He walks over to George, Mr Carver is a big, bald, African geezer, not big as In fat but big as in muscular. He always wears stylish white suits, brown shirt, Sassello tanned brown leather shoes, along with fur felt brown fedora hat. He sits down opposite George, which puts his phone on the table. They finger snap handshake, Mr Carver takes his hat off, placing it to his left.

The chef shouts over asking "All healthy Carve? Got time for a cuppa?"

Mr Carver responds saying "Tea please man, all healthy here, how's yourself?"

The chef responds saying "Yeah all healthy here."

George puts his empty coffee cup up in the air while saying "I will take that second one please chef."

A woman walking past being nosy, looking in, must think that George is raising his cup to her because, she puts her hand up with a puzzled expression as she rushes past, George grins at her misunderstandings, but his eyes soon notice another thing across the street, which is Luke walking towards the bus stops.

His concentration on Luke is soon broken by Mr Carver.

Asking "Any news yet on who killed the boss?"

George responds saying "Not yet bro, the first place I went to only landed me with a dead body, like I need them, the only time I need them is completing contracts."

Mr Carver responds asking "Yeah I heard Tomas Is dead, man is it true that Pinpoint shot through a peephole?"

Two builder to their left get up, to leave on their way they both say "Thanks", "Cheers."

"Have a good one lads!" Comes from the chef that's chopping some lettuce fast in the kitchen, beside the flat top grill, getting ready for the late afternoon folks that need feedings, lettuce that will be used for salads along with baguettes.

George responds "Ahh bro you should of seen it, right through the peephole straight between the guys eyes."

Mr Carver responds asking "Certainty lives up to his name, so you got anything for me?"

George nods as he pulls a brown envelope out from the inside of his suit jacket, passes it to him.

The chef walks over with their drinks, placing them down on the table.

He asks "I know it still might be a sensitive subject, but who is in charge now?"

"We all are, the only difference is all of the contracts come to me first, then I have the privilege to share them out fitting the ability that is required, since day dot I spent it under the boss, he taught me everything I know now."

The chef placing his hand on George's shoulder while saying "Yeah he was a great man, got big shoes to fill Georgie."

He taps his hand on his shoulder once after walks back into the kitchen.

George says to Mr Carver "If you think you need someone for the job, then let me know, I personally think Flames would be fitting, but as you know If you do use him or another member, you split your fifty percent with them fairly."

Mr Carver responds "Yeah standard rate, I will let you know when I have a look in privacy."

George picks his cup up to drink while they carry on talking.

Luke steps onto a bus, in front of him an elderly Indian lady's showing her bus pass.

"Thank you driver." Comes from the elderly lady.

Luke shows his day rider, the drivers eyes scan the date, which is the todays date, he nods to the chunky bus driver In exchange he nods back. Luke heads to the back of the bus, walking past filled seats with different types of multi cultural folks, sitting within them, som old, some young. Two Italian teen ladies get on the bus, they walk upstairs of the double decker, speaking in their mother tongue, as Luke sits down at the back near the window. He sits observing everything around him, the bus doors shut, as it's pulling away from the towns stop, to go through its daily route again. His eyes flicks to a pair of elderly ladies, sitting beside each other with their filled shopping trolleys, in front of them that they are holding on to, as they are nattering but imagine being young with their amount of wisdom, personally I wish I had my wisdom when I was younger, I would of done a lot of shit different but that's hindsight for ya. Luke's eyes flicks to a younger lad, about fourteen years old sitting beside his mother, how does Luke know that because he just heard him call her mum. I personally don't neither does Luke for that matter, or anyone I associate myself with judge someone by the way they look or the clothes they're wearing, because we come from the real world where we didn't have much so what we got we shared, I can't tell you the amount of times I wanted to come home to see my mum, give her a kiss on her cheek, then give her a nice amount of money so she wouldn't have to worry about the many different types of taxes there is, let alone needing money for other things like food to keep ourselves alive, It used to frustrate me seeing my mum also my family struggle to keep their heads above water, but I suppose that's the way they keep the poor well poorer so the rich become richer anyway I shouldn't get myself started because I won't stop telling them they are greedy self centered cunts.

Luke presses the button, as the bus is near his stop but is stopped by traffic lights, Luke takes this time to make his way up to the front of the bus but on his way, he stops off at the young lad, his mum looking out of the window, you can see their has been struggle in their lives. As the bus moves forward again Luke takes five hundred quid out of his pocket, he passes It to the young lad.

He whispers "Treat your mum lad."

The young lad takes the money off Luke, smiling at each other, Like carries on walking to get off from the bus, it stopping at Its designated stop, the doors open.

Luke says to the driver "Thank you sir, have a good day."

The driver responds saying "You're welcome, you too sir."

Luke looks back at the young lad that is explains what happened to his mum, that is holding the cash, Luke gets off the bus, smiling to himself walking left, parallel to the bus he looks at the woman with her son still on the bus, she mouths to Luke "Thank you." Blowing him a kiss. Luke smiles along with winking at the woman, as he carries on walking through this council estate towards his mother's home.

George still sitting within the café, chatting with Mr Carver still when a guy called Jake walks in. A local junkie not for me to judge I get paid to cook sexy food, but you can tell he Is a type of addict that would suck your dick for a rock or a line of coke, dressed In tattered clothes, dirty face also just dirty overall, most probably from sleeping in houses of squalor with squatters or others junkies. George keeping an eye on Jake as he sips his coffee, because he has had a couple of run-ins with this "Rat bastard" (George's words not mine) before, he will do anything to get his hands on anything that's worth cash to buy more drugs, what is it that George calls him? Oh yeah that's it a "Smack head magpie."

He sits down beside Mr Carver, that tells him "Keep your hands on the table, if you steal from me I will brake your fingers, one by one then crush both of your hands."

Jake responds in his thick Scottish accent "I understand pal."

Jake carries on to say to George "I'm sorry to hear about your boss, getting killed."

George responds asking "Who said he was murdered?"

Jake placing his hands flat on the table while responding "Just word on the grapevine."

George responds asking "Any word on the grapevine on who pulled the trigger?"

Jake's jaw swinging like a fighting boxer with his back against the ropes, making sure he doesn't get caught with a punch that will turn his lights out, while his fingers creeping towards

George's mobile that is laying on the table beside his coffee table.

Jake starts to express his words as he responds a

Saying "I heard that a civilian approached a mob out of town, he personally went out of his way to put the hit on your's two boss."

His hand expressions are just a cover to distract their eyes so he can steal his phone, but George's eyes are always scanning, because George knows the devils in every detail. *Slowly, slowly catchy monkey.**Smash!* George gripping his coffee cup handle, but the mug smashing Into the side of Jakes gurning jaw, coffee rocking, spilling out of the cup, shards of cup slowly exploding around his face, some shards cut deep into Jake's jaw, as he is flung backwards dropping George's phone about three inches off the table, George's hand cushioning his phone from hitting the table screen down.*Back to natural speed.* Jake falls off his chair with a few smaller shards of cup in his mug, blood leaking from his wounds, down his dirty cheek. Everyone that is in the café suddenly turns to look at what's the commotion, they eventually go back to minding their own business but not before...

Chef shouts out an order from within the kitchen "There best not be no fucking fighting out there!"

George shouts back asking "Sorry chef, the rubbish is getting taken out now, can you make me another coffee please? Jakes face seems to have broke my cup."

George continues to say to Jake then Carver "You did get told what would happen if you tried to steal. Bro can you take him out please, I will see you later."

Mr Carver shakes George's hand *Click* after Mr Carver picks up his hat, placing it where it's made for, his head.

Mr Carver says "See you later bro, love."

George responds saying "Love bro."

Mr Carver puts the chairs in under the table after picking Jake up from the scruff of his dirty hoody, dragging him out of the café, see if that was me or you that got smashed in the face with a mug, it would hurt like walking over glass barefooted, but for a junkie Jake, I'm sure his jaw was numb like having a tooth pulled out from a dentist.

Luke walks through his mum's homes front door, he Is faced with a normal sight, no one to greet him, so he takes his coat off, the stairs are in front of him, a hallway beside them with a door but it is blocked by the other side because of the fridge freezer in front of that, underneath the stairs though Is a chest freezer, he hangs his coat on the bannister, he turns walking through the door beside the front door, which...

Takes him Into the living room, which is you know a standard childhood family living room, it's got a flatscreen T.V, a light brown comfy sofa along with two matching chair, various family pictures scattered around of them as kids throughout their childhood. A glass coffee table with a swirly black patter running through, in the middle of the room, which sits on top navy blue carpet, that to be honest has seen better days, but to be honest it's old also his mum isn't made of money. But within these walls are a lot of memories that have been lived between both of their childhoods. Now I know you are wondering so ask me, both? Yeah his along with his half sisters Stephanie, but she Is at secondary school, also there is a six years age difference between them but that doesn't overly matter because you most probably won't meet her also that Is Neil's daughter, well obviously it's Luke's mums daughter also, not that they all never got along but like any good family, there is always some raised voices also slamming of doors when there own way wasn't an option.

Luke walks through the living room towards a set of white double doors which separate the living room from the dining room.

Luke calls out "Mum did you get my text!"

He walks into the dining room, the living room window over his shoulder, which has net curtains draped in front of them, some more photos in frames, moments captured in his history sits on the windowsill, one of his first day of secondary school, in his new school uniform, which was captured just In front of them very windows, I think they even had the same carpet sits in the middle of the windowsill. I suppose all we have is the footsteps that we have already taken, because nothing In the future Is guaranteed. There is a door to the side which leads Into the kitchen, he opens the door.

His mum stands cooking a lovely meal, that's the first thing that excites Luke's nostrils, with the radio on, as Gemma is listening to a it of Celine Dion, one of her favorite singers, well it has to be said she has a beautiful voice, Celine that Is, not Gemma well her voice isn't too bad I have heard worst.

Luke says asking "Hi mother, you alright?

She looks up from stirring the steaming saucepan, with its contents reaching boiling point as It starts to well boil, but with each stir It knocks the temperature down a little.

She responds asking or that should say asqueen, "I am in a great mood. You alright sunshine?"

Luke with a smile from ear to ear with a glint in his eye, that Gemma mistake, as she passes him a cup that was In front of the kettle.

Gemma ask "Here you go your cup of tea. You look happy, what's her name?"

Luke chuckles after responds saying "It isn't a lady, I went to check out the key that George gave me at grandads funeral."

Gemma looks puzzled as she asks "You are calling him grandad now?"

From his back pocket Luke pulls out the other five hundred pounds, he smacks it down on the counter.

Luke responds saying "That is for you mum, you can treat yourself to a spar day also some new clothes as long as it goes on you, not Neil. Yes he is my grandfather, he might not of been around which I believe now was for a good reason but when you leave someone ten million, it means he must of thought about me also loved me enough."

Gemma responds asking "I never lied about your grandad or what he done, the question in my love what are you going to do with that money?"

Luke responds saying "I will do good with It, I have already gave five hundred to a homeless man, another five hundred to a kid to treat his mother."

His mum responds saying "I know you will do good, you are a saint."

Luke takes a swig of his tea while, walking over to the sink, looking through the net curtain to their back garden, Neil with using his lawnmower, going up to down trying to get them lines on the grass like you see at football pitches. Luke takes another swig of his tea, putting his cup on the side, oh yeah by the way Luke texts his hum to put the kettle on when he was on the bus, after he walks over to his mum hugging her, giving her a kiss on her cheek.

During the night time when most people are sleeping, George is walking through a rundown corridor, of a hotel. Towards the double white doors, which are located at the end of this corridor, pictures within their frames are not hanging on the walls straight anymore, glass smashed out, shards lay on the ground even more broken up because of the different type shoes, overtime stepping on the glass. Wallpaper on both sides of this corridor, cream curls lay stripped away on the same type of fluffy carpet, you know what type of fluffy carpet I mean, I personally would have it In my own home, that feels sexy on your barefoot, wouldn't want to walk over this carpet barefoot though, maybe when It was a hotel. Before George enters through the double doors that have a gold plaque with 'Enter' in black etched within, with his forearm he pushes the door open....

George walks in to the kitchen of this hotel, which has been taken over by mobsters, the leader is called Two finger Terrance. George's ears are greeted to muffled groans of pain, as a guy is draped across the grubby floor, a strip of black masking tape, masked over his mouth. Terrance has got ahold of the guys wrist, spreading his index finger along with middle finger from the rest of the guys fingers. *Whack.* Terrance's machete slices through both of the separated fingers, blood squirts out, the muffled groans of pain gaining intensity. Now that is the reason why he Is called Two Finger Terrance because as you can see from both of the guys hands, both of them fingers are missing, blood covering the metal counter, the fingers blood soaked in the pool of blood. Terrance is cleaning his custom machete with a grubby tea towel. A couple of guys are cooking drugs with motorbike bandannas covering their mouths, to protect themselves from the fumes, also you know Co-Vid 19 Is still at large. Now if you are wondering why he cuts them two fingers off, it is because the trigger finger so they can't shoot him to get revenge, also the middle finger is because the said subject disrespect him, it is a mark that has become known within this world, If seen by other mobsters they know Terrance has gotten you.

George says "Terrance, I thought you was a chef before all of this, you know for raw meat it's a red board, also you should know chopping on metal will dull your blade."

Terrance looks over, a smile forms on his face showing a couple of gold teeth.This mob is known for not wearing a top, Terrance Is a slim fella with dreadlocks, covered in different types of tattoos, along with scars one comes from a bullet wound, near his heart which give birth to his signature trademark, but the rest of the scars come from knife revenge attacks, I am sure you have worked it out for yourself, but if you haven't Terrance is of Caribbean descent. He pulls up his dark jeans, while walking over to George.

He says to his guys which are dotted around the kitchen, "Get rid of him man."

He shakes George's right hand while asking, "How's it going my brother?"

George responds asking "Well you know how It is, how's everything going with you?"

Two of Terrance's henchmen drag the groaning guy away, leaving a trail of blood, saying that this floor used to be sparkling white, I remember coming to this hotel when it was fully functioning, I was a chef within these walls, the head chef Is the best I have ever worked with. There is several dried blood swiped tracks across the floor, this one bringing moisture to another one which was made previously.

Terrance responds saying "Yeah all good man, I heard you payed a visit to Tomas."

George responds saying "I did, I had an incline he knew something."

Terrance responds saying "Fair enough man, well you know I don't know anything, I would've called you."

George responds saying "This isn't that business but I know you would."

Terrance smacks hands with George after asks "You want a cup?"

George nods after saying "Please."

George walks out of the kitchen, towards the bar that used to be filled with guests of the hotel, followed by Terrance.

The next day Luke Is wearing his casual clothes, standing outside of a small tailor shop, with two suited up mannequins in the shop window, by the looks of It, the shop seems of plentiful style. Luke pushing the gold handle down, the sign to let customers know whether It Is open or closed, swings with the door opening, walking in.

Luke closes the door behind him. The first thing he also yourself will notice is a noise that resembles a chirping bird, as he looks at the elderly grey bushy haired fella, even his mustache is grey, but it is twirled at each end, behind the counter, over his shoulder is a doorway, with the light on but can't see anything of Interest because it's too the rooms left side. He must be wearing a suit which he has tailored for himself. There is the shops selling contend scattered around on mannequins, or just suit jackets hanging up. To the elderly fella's left, two dark brown leather sofas facing each other, a glass coffee table in the middle separating them, some magazines stacked neatly In a pile on its right side, two top hat cup coasters one on each side.

The elderly fella says asking "Hello sir, how are you doing on this lovely sunny day?"

Luke walks up to the counter as he responds asking "It is a lovely day, I am well, are you? I also got left this key by my grandfather?"

His old eyes twinkle with joy, from behind his halved lenses glasses as he smiles at Luke, as he takes his glasses off, folding a temple arm with the other he hooks it to his chest pocket, while closes his sales record book, with his black fountain pen acting as his bookmark, he grabs his carved wooden cane, walking around his shops wooden cash registers counter, talking of tills he has one of them antique gold cash register.

The elder fella responds saying "I am very well, thanks for asking young man, I have been waiting for you, but you know sorry to hear of your grandads passing. A fine man always gave me good business."

Luke responds asking "Was he? Tell me more as I have never met him."

The elderly fella responds saying "My name is Mr Ernest Mould, that key is for a suit that your grandfather, had me tailor for you."

Luke responds asking "How did he know what my size was going to be."

Mr Devise responds saying "Well with such intelligence, I will tell you what he told me, as long as he isn't a fat man, he will be this size, he designed a mannequin on what size you will be, by what I can remember he isn't wrong."

Mr Devise changes his view by stepping a couple of steps to the left, lining said suited mannequin in the background with Luke.

Luke looks over his shoulder seeing the mannequin.

He asks "Is that the suit?"

Earnest responds saying "No my dear boy, it has been put away, it has its own box, a very nice box if I might say so myself."

Luke asks "Did you make the box?"

He nods after takes the key from Luke after walks back around the counter.

Mr Devise carries on saying to ask "That however is the mannequin. Would you like a hot beverage my dear boy?"

While he pulls a oak box off from one of the counter's shelves.

Luke responds saying "Yes please, I will have a tea with two sugars."

He places It on the counter, it has a metal plaque family crest in the middle of the oak box, while Mr Mould is unlocking the box with the key that Luke gave him. He calls to someone that is in the back room "Can you make two cups of tea please Miss Hem? Mr Luke will have his like mine my dear lady!"

The noise of a bird chirping suddenly stops, a young lady with tied up blond hair, pokes her head around the doorway, beautiful lips painted with red lipstick, Luke stuck looking at her beautiful blue eyes, which lock onto Luke's eyes, a smile covers her face, as she responds saying "Sure can Mr Mould."

She disappears back into the small room, you can hear running water, filling the kettle up, that is clicked on, warming the water within.

Earnest says "Thank you dear."

He carries on saying "Come here my dear boy, you have to open It."

Luke joins Earnest on the other side of the counter, he takes a look in the side room on his way around. Seeing Miss Hem wearing a ladies dark grey skirt suit with dark grey heels, beautiful legs up to her ass, she is putting the tea bags into three posh cups that are sitting on their sets saucers. Luke turns his attention to the large oak box.

Mr Mould says "That is your family crest, a crest your grandfather was proud of."

Luke rubs his hand over his families crest, after lifts the box's lid up to reveal the chosen suit for him to try on.

Luke steps out of a changing room, which are situated at the shops back, there are two side by side, Luke turns the rooms light off, you know because electricity isn't cheep. He steps out closing the espresso oak door, the same as the one beside. Mr Mould Is sitting on the sofa, with his back to his shops entrance.

Luke responds saying "I look nice, scrub up alright, considering I don't really wear suits."

Luke walks towards him while Mr Device takes a sip from his tea, placing it back on his coaster.

As he says "Your grandfather had a good eye for measurements."

Luke says "Come on now, you did make It as well."

Luke picking his tea, slurping his tea, noticing this slurping of his tea like a common man, is starting to wind M Mould up, him being prim to proper. Luke goes to do it again, Mr Mould standing to walk over to Luke, Earnest is quick to interrupt him by saying "Look at them shoes, they are beautiful, black with a red tint, it matches the black with red pinstripes suit perfectly, my boy I have been waiting for ages to see this suit."

Luke says "It is nice also comfy but I will need another suit when this one needs to be washed, you don't have to make it I will take what you have got already made."

"Oh no you don't wash this suit, you have it dry cleaned I will give you a card for an excellent one. Come with me my boy, I will show you what suits I have got in your size."

As Mr Mould stops admiring their handy word, as he turns, walking near the front of his shop, with Luke following.

Luke says "Something that will go with these shoes, they are comfy mate, like tailored to my feet."

Luke has a quiet slurp of his tea.

A man tied with rope, wearing a bloody white t'shirt, leaning over, blood droplet falling from his broken nose, drips onto his blood soaking jeans, a chunk from under his right eye has been sliced off, thanks to the handiwork of Mr Carver, which is standing beside the tied up guy, in the guys living room. Mr Carver cleans his blade on the outside of this guys leg, blood seeps in to his jeans, his carpet is fucked.

Mr Carver requests the information he needs again, but the in pain panting man keeps his silence. Well that is until Flames puts a blue bottled blow torch In his face, torching his cheek as the flame, starts sizzling away the skin, melting away, The guy of course loudly expresses his pain from the burning he is feeling.

He shouts out "Okay, I will talk!"

Flames stops like a kid that is annoyed he has to stop something he finds fun.

Luke is his normal clothes, Mr Mould is the other side of the counter, placing two suits in a bag.

Luke shouts through to the other room "See you later Miss!"

Mr Mould says "Yeah alright lover boy, put your tongue back in your mouth."

Miss Hem shouts back "Bye Sir!"

Luke smiles at Earnest, which cracks a smile.

Luke says asking "I can see why grandad liked you, so you know what this other key is for."

As he holds it up but Mr Mould is quick to take It from Luke's fingertips, as he examines the key closer, after gives it back.

While responding asking "Not sure, is there a clue?"

Luke responds saying "I will have to re-read the letter that Grandad left me."

He takes the bag of suits from Earnests offering hand.

Luke says "Anyway thank you kind sir."

Mr Mould responds saying "Anytime my boy, have a good day."

They shake hands after Luke goes to walk out, as a stocky white fella, dressed in a black tracksuit looks like he likes a scrap. He holds the door open for Luke while saying "There you go old chap."

Luke nods after responds "Thank you, sir."

Luke walks out of the suit tailoring shop turning right, onto the cobblestone pathway, leading both ways with shops also restaurants either side.

Until next time my friend. I salute you if you're a fella, if you're a lady then a hug for you.

Oh this story will definitely be the first story in Free Time Two. But I think my next story will be Earths Framework. Thank you for your time, it is important so choose what you do wisely. Stay safe out there also treat people how you want to be treated.